D0722956

"This lighthearted peek into small-town secrets and rumors carries enough good humor, emotional honesty, plot twists, and recipes to entertain and satisfy."

— *Publishers Weekly*

"A delightful amateur sleuth who is not only exciting but also never melts down."

— *Midwest Book Review*

"Readers will just adore Tally and her no-nonsense attitude. *I Scream, You Scream* is an enjoyable visit to small-town Texas with a helping of murder to boot."

— *Fresh Fiction*

"Watson takes the mystery reader on a wild Texas stampede in *I Scream, You Scream*...Humor abounds and the novel features lively, interesting characters."

— *Gumshoe*

"A deliciously-written cozy mystery that will delight chick lit fans, especially those who like added suspense. There is enough humor and plots twists to keep the characters engaging, and the love story is nicely played with the "did he or didn't he?" thrown in."

— *Chick Lit Plus*

"Wendy Lyn Watson? She writes damn good prose. Her descriptions are vibrant, but not in the least bit florid. Her dialogue sparkles. And the images she paints are so vivid, they practically spring to mind fully formed."

— *Criminal Element*

SCOOP TO KILL

**The Mystery A-la-mode Series
by Wendy Lyn Watson**

I SCREAM, YOU SCREAM (#1)
SCOOP TO KILL (#2)
A PARFAIT MURDER (#3)

SCOOP TO KILL

A Mystery A-la-mode

WENDY LYN WATSON

HENERY PRESS

Copyright

SCOOP TO KILL
A Mystery A-la-mode
Part of the Henery Press Mystery Collection

Second Edition | May 2018

Henery Press, LLC
www.henerypress.com

Trade Paperback ISBN-13: 978-1-63511-368-6
Digital epub ISBN-13: 978-1-63511-369-3
Kindle ISBN-13: 978-1-63511-370-9
Hardcover ISBN-13: 978-1-63511-371-6

Printed in the United States of America

For Cleone.

Thanks for your son and your love.

ACKNOWLEDGMENTS

I am ashamed at how many people I will be leaving out of this list, but let me do what I can. I must, as always, thank my agent, Kim Lionetti, for taking that initial leap of faith with me and for being such a staunch ally for many years now. More recently, Kendel Lynn has taken that leap of faith. I hope I can do them both proud.

On the professional front I have also had incredible moral support from Aimee Hix, Dru Ann Love, Misa Ramirez, and an army of others (okay, they are my friends, too). I am also lucky enough to have a wonderful family who keeps the rest of my life moving—Karen, Mom, Cleone, and Stuart. Finally, in all things and in all ways, I have my husband Peter, who keeps me sane, keeps me laughing, and keeps me focused on being the best person I can be.

One

"I can't even believe that woman is related to me."

"Alice, honey, I hate to tell you, but you and your mama are like two kits in a litter. Hardheaded, tenderhearted, and too smart for your own good." I ran a hand through my hair and sighed. "Too smart for my own good."

Alice folded her arms across her chest and cocked a skinny hip. She still looked more like a child than a woman, and I had a tough time remembering that she was finishing up her first year at Dickerson University. "That is so not true, Aunt Tally. I would never in a million years show up at a formal event looking like a hoochie."

I studied my cousin, Alice's mama, trying to see her through her precocious teenage daughter's eyes. Bree Michaels wore a vibrant pink tank dress that clung to every luscious curve of her statuesque form. A beam of late afternoon sunlight filtered through the atrium windows of Sinclair Hall, brightening her bouffant updo to a glossy maraschino-cherry red. And when she threw her head back and laughed at one of her admirers' quips, her abundant décolletage frothed like freshly whipped cream until I thought she might overflow her D cups. She looked like a sexy strawberry sundae, and the men surrounding her—from adolescents to octogenarians—practically drooled on her three-inch spike heels.

Out of the corner of my eye, I caught Alice tugging on the

cuffs of her prim white cotton dress shirt, and I smothered a chuckle.

"In your mama's defense, the invitation called this shindig a 'reception,' and they're serving barbecue and ice cream. Not exactly black tie and tails."

"You know what I mean," Alice huffed. "You dressed appropriately."

I glanced down at my own outfit, a knee-length black skirt and French blue wrap shirt. "I look like a waitress," I muttered.

"Better a waitress than a call girl."

"Show a little respect, Alice. And cut your mama some slack. She's terrified she's going to embarrass you today."

Alice snorted.

"Seriously. Bree was a hot mess this morning. She tried on three different outfits and spent an hour on her hair, and she was still shaking so bad I thought she'd collapse the minute we walked in here and saw all the posters and displays."

My niece nibbled on her lower lip, and I could see the wheels turning behind eyes as wide and blue as the prairie sky. "Mom's no shrinking violet," she insisted.

"You're right. Bree's cocky as heck when she's on her own turf. When she's singing karaoke at the Bar None or scooping cones at Remember the A-la-mode. But Honors Day on a college campus? Scares the piddle out of her." I wrapped an arm around Alice's scrawny shoulders and pressed a kiss to the silky hair at her temple. "Your mother is so freakin' proud of you, little girl. Just turned seventeen and you're presenting a research project at a prestigious private university? When she was your age, your mama had just gotten hitched to husband number one and was living in a camper in her in-laws' side yard. She doesn't want to hold you back, kiddo."

Alice leaned in to me, and I gave her a little squeeze. Underneath the eighty-pound attitude, she was a great kid.

Before we could get any gooier, a smartly dressed woman emerged from the curtained platform that ran along one side of the atrium and made a beeline for us. I put her somewhere in her early to mid-thirties. Her caramel-colored hair fell just past her angular jaw in a chic asymmetrical bob, and funky tortoiseshell glasses rested on her aquiline nose. As she strode closer, I could see the nubby weave of her ankle-length gray dress and eggplant jacket, maybe linen or hemp. The name tag pinned to her breast read DR. EMILY CLOWPER, DEPARTMENT OF ENGLISH.

"Alice, have you seen Bryan?" she snapped. Like a pit viper on speed, she vibrated with barely controlled energy.

"No, Dr. C.," Alice said. "Reggie said he was still running off programs."

Emily glanced at her watch, clearly irritated. "Figures. Go find him, will you? It's time to get this show on the road."

Alice slipped from under my arm and trotted off without a backward glance.

I held out my hand. "Hi. I'm Tally Jones."

Emily looked at my hand like it was a riddle to be solved before grasping it and giving it a single, bone-wrenching shake.

"You make the ice cream," she said.

I smiled. "Have you tried it? The university is serving cones of honey-vanilla bean, raspberry mascarpone, and chocolate truffle out by the barbecue."

"Diabetic."

"Oh." Alice raved about Emily Clowper's brilliant mind, but she sure couldn't carry a conversation.

She looked at her watch again and sighed.

"Uh, thank you for taking Alice under your wing. She loves working for you."

Emily's mouth softened into something approaching a smile. "The pleasure is mine. This paper she's presenting today on the misogynist subtext of Robinson Crusoe is graduate-level work. I'm not a Freudian, but she's made a compelling case for the island as a symbol of dehumanized female sexuality."

"Oh."

"Her mother?"

"What? Oh, no. Aunt. Well, actually first cousin once removed." One of her eyebrows shot up, and I felt like I'd got caught passing notes in class. "I'm her aunt."

I glanced nervously across the room to where Bree continued to hold court. This woman would make Bree cry.

When I looked back at Emily, her attention had moved to something—or someone—behind me. Now there was no mistaking her smile or the crinkling at the corners of her eyes, the subtle softening of her posture.

"I didn't expect to see you here, Finn," she said.

My heart did a somersault in my chest as I turned to find Finn Harper standing at my shoulder, a camera hanging from a strap around his neck. His mouth curled in a devilish smile, and I couldn't tell whether the heat in his velvet green eyes was for me or for Emily.

Either way, I wanted to curl up in a tiny ball and die.

My relationship with Finn remained uncertain. After a near twenty-year absence, he had returned to Dalliance about six months ago to take care of his ailing mother. A bizarre set of circumstances threw us together, and I flirted with the notion that we'd pick up our teenage romance right where we'd left off.

But, of course, real life didn't have fairy-tale endings. I still needed to unload a lot of baggage from my marriage and divorce, and I struggled to untangle the dreamy memories of my high school heartthrob from the man he had become. Bottom line, we'd both done a lot of living since I broke his heart in the Tasty-Swirl parking lot when I was eighteen.

I still saw him out and about, at the cafés and shops that

circled the courthouse square of Dalliance, Texas, and at the various events he covered as a reporter for the *Dalliance News-Letter*. But every single encounter reduced me to a stammering, gelatinous mess.

Dr. Emily Clowper held out her arms, and Finn stepped awkwardly into her embrace. I couldn't bear to look at him, so I studied her, instead, seeing her this time the way a man would see her. Like the eye doctor switching from one lens to the next, my perception of her shifted from awkward and angular to tall and lithe, from cold and abrupt to smart and edgy.

When Finn stepped back, he looked at me, eyes narrowed and appraising. I prayed I didn't look as miserable as I felt.

"Emily and I met when I lived in Minneapolis," Finn offered.

Her smile widened into an almost girlish grin. "Many years and three moves ago. Back in my wild grad school days."

Finn held up a hand in protest. "Not that long ago. And not that wild."

They both laughed, and I forced myself to join in. No matter how long ago they'd been together, their relationship was more recent than ours. And certainly more wild. Emily Clowper had known Finn as an adult, as a self-sufficient man, a person I'd only recently met.

I tried to find something clever to say. "How convenient that fate landed you both in the same Podunk town," I said, then cringed. Even to my ears, my words sounded bitter. "I mean—"

A piercing scream rang through the room, echoing off the high ceiling and leaving an unnatural stillness in its wake.

Alice.

My legs were moving before my brain even finished the thought, but still I was three steps behind Bree as she sprinted across the tile floor of the atrium in her tight dress and hooker heels. I sensed movement behind me, others running toward the cry of distress, which had now settled into a keening wail.

Ahead of me, Bree took the half flight of steps from the atrium into the main body of Sinclair Hall two at a time, then disappeared through the heavy oak doors propped open for the festivities.

I took the corner onto the first floor in a blind panic and nearly fell over Bree, who'd come to a dead stop, staring in horror at the scene in the hallway.

Alice, our baby girl, stood beneath the harsh fluorescent lights, face the color of chalk, her prim white cotton dress shirt covered in blood.

"Bryan," Alice gasped. "It's Bryan."

She raised one frail arm to point an accusatory finger, bone-white and smeared with gore, toward the open doorway at her side. She looked like a grim apparition from a Shakespearean tragedy, a ghost come to torment the guilty and the damned.

My first thought was that this Bryan person had better run like the wind, because when Bree got her hands on the boy stupid enough to hurt her baby girl, she'd tear him limb from limb. Then Alice took one stumbling step before finding her sea legs and bolting down the hall into her mama's arms. That's when I realized that the blood streaking Alice's shirt was not her own.

By then the guests from the Honor's Day festivities along with a hodgepodge of black-robed faculty and disheveled-looking students, had crowded into the hall around me. A few brave souls, including both Finn and Emily Clowper, rushed forward to peer into the office from which Alice had emerged. A bright red placard with gold lettering hung beside the door: DEPARTMENT OF ENGLISH LANGUAGE AND LITERATURE.

"Someone call 911," Finn yelled, as Emily staggered back and slumped against the corridor wall.

A bluff man in a kelly-green golf shirt and a navy blazer, surely the proud dad of one of the honored students, pushed past me. "I'm a doctor," he declared.

Finn held out a hand to stop him. "I don't think there's anything you can do," he said. "And I don't think the police would want us mucking up their crime scene." He looked past the good doctor's shoulder and caught my gaze.

It seemed murder had come to Dalliance, Texas, once again.

Two

It may be blasphemy to say it here in Texas, but if William Travis and his men had defended the Alamo the way Bree defended Alice that day, General Santa Anna would have scooted back to Mexico with his tail between his legs. I'm telling you, Bree was a sight to behold: half-naked in her skimpy pink sundress, her hair teased seven ways from Sunday, purple-painted toenails peeping from three-inch high strappy silver sandals, and a look in her eyes that could have brought a grown man to his knees.

If, that is, that grown man had been anyone other than Detective Cal McCormack. He'd heard the call come in over the scanner, that twenty-six-year-old doctoral student Bryan Campbell had been bludgeoned to death, apparently with an industrial-sized stapler, but he wasn't on the case. The victim was Cal's nephew, his older sister Marla's boy.

Cal and I go way back, back to summer games of kickball and capture-the-flag. We weren't close anymore, but I knew Cal McCormack as well as anyone. Laid-back, laconic, law-abiding Cal. That afternoon in Sinclair Hall, though, I saw a side of Cal McCormack I'd never seen before.

He was incandescent with fury.

"What the hell happened here?" he bellowed, towering over Alice as she huddled in the shelter of her mother's arms.

Bree angled her body between Alice and the colossal

cowboy and raised her chin to stare him in the eye. "Don't you take that tone with my child, Cal McCormack."

The Cal I knew would be chastened by a southern woman asserting her motherly credentials, would have tipped his hat (metaphorically speaking) and begged pardon. But this new Cal spun like a force of nature.

"Back off, Bree," he barked. "Your child is covered in Bryan's blood, and she's going to tell me why." He took another ominous step, crowding Bree and Alice against the wall. "Now."

I recognized the mulish expression on my cousin's face. Irresistible force had met immovable object, and nothing good could come from that. I decided I ought to wade in to prevent further bloodshed.

Carefully, I placed a gentle hand on Cal's arm. His muscles vibrated like a tuning fork beneath my fingers.

"Cal," I whispered.

"Not now, Tally," he growled.

"Cal," I said more forcefully. "You're not going to get anywhere like this. Why don't you walk with me a minute?"

He shook my hand off, but he backed away from Bree and Alice.

I followed as he stalked down the hall a few yards, then stopped and dropped onto one of the low benches that lined the walls. He scrubbed his face with his square, long-fingered hands.

"Christ a-mighty," he sighed. "What am I going to tell Marla?"

I sat next to him, perching gingerly on the edge of the bench. "I'm so sorry, Cal."

He looked down the hall, gaze resting briefly on Alice and Bree before focusing on the doorway to the English Department office. Parents, students, and faculty had cleared away, leaving a harried knot of uniformed law enforcement: Dickerson

University police, Dalliance police, and a couple of representatives of the Lantana County Sheriff's Department. A muscle in Cal's jaw bunched and released, as though he were chewing over a tough thought.

"Dammit," he muttered. "I can't even work the case. Can't do shit."

Cal and I hadn't spoken much over the last twenty years, but I felt like I knew him pretty well. Cal's grandma and mine were neighbors, and Cal and I had grown up within biking distance of each other. As kids, we'd matched wits with one another over games of Risk and Monopoly, played on the same peewee softball team, and dunked each other at the community swimming pool.

In high school, the fact that Cal had more money and was way cooler than me suddenly started to matter. He still came to my rescue on occasion—like when my mama got plastered and threatened to drive to Tulsa and shoot my daddy with Grandma Peachy's shotgun—but we didn't go to the same parties or hang out with the same kids anymore. Then, as adults, he'd gone into the military and I'd gotten married, so we didn't really cross paths much until the trouble of the autumn before. Still, those lazy summer evenings of lightning bugs and flashlight tag bound us together as surely as blood.

Cal acted. He fought, he seized, he saved, he fixed, he did. Having to sit on the sidelines while his family absorbed such a blow would kill him.

"Marla's gonna need you by her side," I said. "That's the best place in the world for you to be."

Once again, I laid my hand on his forearm. This time, he didn't push me away. Instead, he covered my hand with his own.

"Detective McCormack?"

Cal and I jumped apart as though we'd been burned.

Emily Clowper stood before us, Finn at her side. Tentatively she extended a hand. "I'm Dr. Clowper. I was on Bryan's committee. I'm so sorry for your loss."

Cal bolted to his feet. He gave Emily's hand a hard stare, but made no move to take it. His mama would have had a fit and dropped dead on the spot if she'd witnessed her son behaving so rudely.

"I know who you are," Cal said, something dark and dangerous in his voice. "And I don't imagine you're sorry at all."

What little color was left in Emily's face drained away, and she let her proffered hand fall to her side.

"I beg your pardon?" she said.

"What's happened to your hearing now that Bryan's gone, huh?"

Blood rushed to Emily's waxen cheeks, staining them a hectic crimson.

"Detective McCormack, university counsel has advised me not to discuss Bryan's allegations or the upcoming hearing with anyone."

"Sounds mighty convenient," Cal snapped.

Emily shook her head. "Hardly," she said. She looked like she was about to argue further with Cal, but Finn placed a restraining hand on her arm. He leaned in to whisper something in her ear. Whatever he said, it clicked. She heaved an impatient sigh, but then visibly collected herself.

"Once again, Detective McCormack, I'm sorry for your loss." Without waiting for an answer, she walked away, turning the corner at the end of the hall and disappearing.

Cal watched her go, jaw hard and eyes harder, before turning on his heel and storming off in the opposite direction.

Once he was out of earshot, I faced Finn. "What the heck was that all about?"

He fidgeted with his camera strap, and I wasn't sure he'd answer me. But then he shrugged. "It's a long story," he said.

"Basically, Emily failed Bryan on some exam, and he claimed that she did it in retaliation because he refused her, uh, romantic advances."

Sexual. Finn meant "sexual advances." I tried to imagine the abrupt, prickly woman I'd met today making a pass at a younger man. It seemed far-fetched. But given the looks she'd exchanged with Finn, she clearly wasn't a nun.

"That sounds pretty serious," I said weakly.

"Apparently so," Finn said. "Bryan had retained a lawyer and was threatening to sue the school, so there was a lot of pressure on the administration to act. The university had an administrative hearing scheduled for the week after next, after the semester ended. If the university determined Bryan was telling the truth, Emily probably would have lost her job. Finding another academic position after something like that would have been downright impossible. And there aren't that many other jobs out there for people with Ph.D.'s in English."

"Wow." I searched Finn's face, but his expression remained flat, impassive. "And now that Bryan's dead?"

He shrugged again. "I'm not sure. Certainly no lawsuit. And from what Emily said, which wasn't much, Bryan didn't have any evidence. It was just her word against his. And he was lying."

"According to Emily."

He met my eyes, and I saw the conviction in his gaze. "Yes, according to Emily," he conceded. "But she was telling the truth."

"You're sure?"

"I'm sure. Emily's not perfect, but she's a straight arrow. She'd never abuse her power over a student. And if she did, she wouldn't be able to cover it up. There isn't a deceptive bone in her body."

"Hmmm." In my experience, everyone kept secrets.

Everyone lied, if the stakes were high enough.

Emily Clowper certainly had enough at stake to lie. But did she have enough at stake to kill?

Three

By Monday morning, news of the murder at Dickerson University had spread like a west Texas brush fire, igniting latent town animosity into a full-fledged inferno of speculation and name-calling. And rightly or wrongly, Dr. Emily Clowper was strapped to a stake right in the middle of it all.

Down-home, no-nonsense, small-town pride was as integral to life in Dalliance, Texas as the gas-rich shale that runs beneath the arid north Texas soil. Big box stores and suburban strip malls were cropping up out on FM 410, but the heart of the town still beat in the tiny courthouse square. Folks from outside Texas would sometimes comment that the courthouse square reminded them of a medieval castle, guarded by a moat of one-way streets and knights in white pickup trucks. The town barely tolerated the highfalutin university on the best of days, and with trouble brewing on campus, the pickups were closing ranks.

Rants about an East Coast intellectual preying on a hometown boy and ivory-towered eggheads closing ranks to protect their own filled the Op-Ed page of the *Dalliance Newsletter* (never mind that Emily Clowper was from Minnesota or that Dickerson had acted with lightning speed to place her on administrative leave pending the resolution of the police investigation). Meanwhile, the *Dickerson Daily* lamented the lack of objectivity of the Dalliance PD and fretted about a rush to judgment that might ruin the career of a promising young scholar (never mind that Cal McCormack had been barred from anything to do with the investigation or that the authorities officially denied that Emily was a suspect).

Alice had no trouble choosing sides.

"It's not fair, Aunt Tally," she said as she lugged a two-gallon tub of our new "Flamin' Hot Chile-Pineapple" ice cream out of the walk-in freezer. "Dr. Clowper didn't do anything wrong, but she's being punished anyway."

We were getting ready to open the Remember the A-la-mode—stocking the freezer, balancing the till, heating the sundae sauces—before Alice headed off to class. "Most people wouldn't consider a paid vacation 'punishment,'" I responded as I dropped a metal pot of fudge into the water bath and turned on the heat. I might have had my doubts about Emily's innocence, but I knew better than to argue the point with Alice.

She heaved the bucket of ice cream into the empty spot in the display freezer with a tiny grunt. Alice didn't weigh more than a buck ten soaking wet, but she worked like a dray horse. "It's not a vacation. It's a banishment. They won't even let her finish her classes this semester, and she can't teach the May term class she was scheduled for."

"May term?" I asked. "Is that like summer school?"

"Sort of. It's a little short term in between the regular semester and summer school. Just three weeks, but each class meets for three hours a day, five days a week."

"That sounds horrible," I muttered.

Alice laughed. "It's not fun, either for students or teachers. But Dr. Clowper was going to teach the short term so she could travel the rest of the summer."

"Must be nice," Bree said. "Now she can leave even sooner."

"No, now she probably can't go at all. She needed the income from the May term class to fund a research trip to the East Coast later this summer. Massachusetts and Washington."

Bree, who had been counting out the change drawer under her breath, paused in the middle of a stack of fives. "Massachusetts? She writes about books. Don't they have books here?"

Alice let the door to the display freezer drop with a thud. "Jeez, Mom," she snapped. "She's working on a book about the political subtext of Emily Dickinson's poetry, and she needs access to the collection of her letters and diaries in Amherst and to information about her father's term in Congress. Without the summer teaching money, she'll have to get a grant to fund the trip. And grant money is really, really tough to get."

"Sor-ry," Bree drawled.

Alice rolled her eyes, but she seemed mollified. "It's a big deal," she said. "Dr. Clowper's up for tenure next year, and she needs this book to be done and published if she wants to keep her job. It's all about tenure, you know."

A flicker of wistfulness clouded Bree's expression. We both wanted Alice to have a good education and all the opportunities that brought with it. But the bottom line was that Alice was entering a world Bree and I knew little about. Our little girl was vanishing right before our eyes, being transformed into a sophisticated stranger.

"How do you know so much about the nitty-gritty of Emily Clowper's job situation? As in her precise situation at this moment?" I asked, sliding a canister of salted caramel sauce in next to the fudge.

Alice's shoulders jerked, and she turned toward the sink. She cranked on the faucet to wash her hands, and for a second the hollow roar of water on metal made talking impossible.

I waited until she snatched up a towel and knocked the tap closed with her elbow. "Alice?"

Bree had slid the cash drawer closed and was watching her daughter with narrowed eyes.

Alice sighed. "Okay. I didn't tell you because I knew you'd be all crazy about it, but I talked with Dr. Clowper last night."

"You what?" Bree barked.

"It's no big deal. I went over so that we could talk about my paper—"

Bree cut her off. "'Went over'? You mean to her house?"

"Yeah. It's really no big deal. She's had over all the students who are doing independent studies with her so we can workshop our projects. We order pizza and sit around her living room. It's just more comfortable than meeting in her office and quieter than a coffee shop or whatever."

"Were these other kids at her house last night?"

Alice looked at her feet for a moment, before raising her chin and facing her mother squarely. "No. I went by myself. Dr. Clowper had sent us a mass e-mail saying she wasn't allowed to come to campus until everything gets resolved, and I was worried about her." She tucked her sleek strawberry hair behind her ear. "I tried to get some of the other kids to come with me, to show our solidarity."

"But they were all too smart to say 'yes,' huh?" Bree shook her head. "Well, you're not gonna do that again."

Alice's jaw slid to the side, like she was chewing on gristle. "Actually, I am. Dr. Clowper isn't allowed on campus, and they even put a hold on her account so she can't access the library or the school computer network from home. So she gave me the key to her office, and I promised her I would stop by a couple of times a week so I can bring her things she needs for her work."

Bree gasped in outrage, but Alice pressed on. "I want to show her that we don't all think she's some sort of criminal." She set her small fists on her hips. "Because she's not."

Bree matched her daughter's belligerent stance, so I sidled up to her, ready to intervene if things got too nasty. After all, I had to unlock the store in a few minutes, and their domestic dispute wouldn't be good for business.

"She's not a criminal," Bree mocked. "And do you have anything other than her word for that?"

"Yes," Alice said. "I have my own good judgment."

That took a little of the starch out of Bree's spine. "I still don't like it," she insisted. Even if she weren't a suspect—"

"She's not a suspect."

Bree raised her hand. "Even if she weren't a suspect," she repeated, "I think it's weird for you to go to a teacher's house, especially by yourself. If there was any way for you to drop your classes this late in the semester, I wouldn't even let you on that campus. I sure as heck don't want you spending one-on-one time with a possible murderer."

Alice opened her mouth, then snapped it closed. She shook her head as she stripped her apron off. "I have to go to class," she muttered, holding up a hand to fend off any potential argument, "with hundreds of other students in broad daylight. We can talk about this later."

"There's nothing to talk about," Bree insisted.

"Whatever."

Nothing got under Bree's skin more than that one dismissive little word. She tensed up again, ready to have it out with her troublesome child.

"Let it go, Bree," I hissed.

Bree shot me an irritated glance, but Alice was already on her way out the back door, a backpack that probably weighed as much as she did slung over one shoulder.

"Can you believe that?" Bree huffed as the door banged shut.

Bree snorted. "Going to that woman's house without so much as a by-your-leave? I thought I raised that child better than that."

I smothered a laugh. "She's more like you every day." Bree

shot me a disbelieving look. It killed me that neither mother nor daughter could see how much alike they were. "She's fiercely loyal, listens to her gut, stubborn as a mule, shall I go on?"

I walked to the front door, flipped the OPEN sign, and threw the deadbolt. Late April weather in North Texas is unpredictable, but the local news promised sun and highs in the eighties for the day. With any luck, the A-la-mode would be jumping by lunch.

"Listen," I said. "Whether you like it or not, Alice is going to stand by her teacher. And you can't watch her every minute of every day."

"Wanna bet?"

I let the laughter escape this time. "For what it's worth, Finn thinks pretty highly of this lady, and he's a good judge of character."

Bree arched an eyebrow, and I knew she was itching to press me about Finn and Emily, but she showed uncharacteristic restraint.

"Why don't you compromise?" I suggested. "Tell Alice that she can meet with Dr. Clowper, but they have to meet here. On neutral territory."

Bree snapped a clean apron over her head.

"Not a bad plan. Though I'm not sure either one of us is 'neutral' toward that woman."

Four

Much to Bree's surprise, Alice and Emily both agreed to meet at the A-la-mode. Much to my surprise, Emily brought Finn Harper with her.

I watched through my plate glass storefront as Finn waited patiently on the sidewalk, hands shoved deep in the pockets of his rumpled khakis, while Emily locked a pink bicycle to a parking meter. Her short flippy purple skirt and ballet-necked white T-shirt showed off a lithe figure that her long linen dress had concealed when I first met her. With a canvas tote bag slung across her body and a pair of earth sandals on her feet, she looked like she could be a college student herself.

Finn held the door for both Alice and Emily, and they filed to the back of the store.

"Anyone want ice cream?" I asked as they settled down around one of my wrought iron café tables. Bree crossed behind them to the door to lock up for the day and Kyle Mason, my only nonfamily employee, slouched by the restroom door, watching Alice's every move with a blend of longing and animosity peculiar to moody teenagers. Poor Kyle teetered right on the brink of adulthood, but Alice, his crush, had already entered the grown-up world of college. He chafed at being left behind.

"No, thanks," Alice said, as she rooted around in her backpack.

"You know I can't resist your ice cream, Tally," Finn said

with a wink. "Bring me something tasty."

I looked at Emily. She stared back, her brow furrowed in confusion. "Diabetic. Just water."

Ah yes, no ice cream for Dr. Emily Clowper. She probably ran marathons, too, or did that hot yoga stuff.

As though he read my mind, Finn piped up. "Don't let Emily fool you. She has a sweet tooth."

She glared at him. "I like sweets," she conceded, "but they'll kill me. Literally. So I resist temptation."

"Hmmm. I seem to recall a certain evening at Ciao Bella that involved multiple desserts."

Emily blushed. "All tiramisu. Every time I'm near a piece of the stuff, I absolutely inhale it, and then spend the evening shooting up extra insulin to compensate." She lowered her eyes. "Some temptations are simply too great."

Eww. I really didn't want to be privy to this conversation.

I ducked behind the counter and dished up two scoops of cherry-vanilla, Finn's favorite flavor, and topped it with a ladle of warm bittersweet chocolate fudge and a dollop of whipped cream.

Bree filled a glass with ice water for Emily, popped open a can of Diet Dr. Pepper for herself, and slid Alice a can of the full-sugar variety. I handed Finn his ice cream and smiled as he tucked in with gusto.

"Em," Finn said around a mouth full of my French pot ice cream, "you have no idea what you're missing."

I tried to ignore the pang I felt at Finn's use of Emily's pet name. It was none of my business how long they'd dated, how serious they'd been, how much tiramisu he'd fed her, or even whether they were back together. I tried to ignore that pang, but if we're being brutally honest, I failed.

"So what's the scoop?" Bree asked as she took a swig of her soda.

Alice piped up. "Dr. Landry asked Reggie to cover Dr. Clowper's May term American Lit class, and Reggie asked me today if I'd be willing to work as a TA."

Kyle laughed. "T and A?" he scoffed. "Not sure you're qualified Ally."

Alice glared at him. "TA. Teaching assistant. Grading and helping students who are struggling and stuff. Usually, that's a job for graduate students and sometimes senior undergrads, but the department is a little shorthanded"—she glanced sheepishly at Emily—"and it's short notice. I mean the class starts the week after next, right after spring finals. I'm local, and I aced the class last fall. Reggie said I'd be a natural."

Something about the way Alice said Reggie's name, a smug note of satisfaction in her voice as she repeated his praise, made me wonder whether this Reggie person might be a little bit handsome. Out of the corner of my eye, I saw Kyle's teasing smile turn into a glower, suggesting he'd noticed the very same thing.

"Who's this Reggie person?" I asked.

"He's another graduate student," Alice said. "He and Bryan shared an office."

"Reggie's ABD," Emily added. "All but dissertation," she clarified. "He's completed all of his course work and just has to finish his research and defend his dissertation, and then he'll graduate. He'll be a great mentor for Alice."

Bree looked dubious. "I don't know if this is such a good idea," she said.

"Come on, Mom," Alice wheedled. "I can still pull my weight around the shop. It will look great on my resume, and I'll even get paid."

Emily nodded. "It would be a great opportunity for Alice, so I suggested her name to Reggie." I caught the subtle emphasis Emily put on the word "I," and by the way she stiffened, I guessed Bree had, too. Everyone in the room knew that Alice had this opportunity because of Emily's largesse. "Alice will do a wonderful job," she added more graciously, "and it will free up Reggie to work on his dissertation."

I knew my cousin well enough to realize that, at this point, if Emily had said the earth was round, Bree would cry "flat!" By the time Emily finished her argument, Bree was already shaking her head.

Alice's face set in a mulish expression, ready to duke it out, but Bree tipped her head toward Emily and Finn. "We'll talk about it later."

Alice huffed and rolled her eyes, but Bree didn't budge.

"What are they saying about Bryan around campus?" Finn asked, trying to bring the conversation back to more neutral territory. Though I suppose talk of a murder shouldn't really be considered "neutral."

"Nothing interesting," Alice reported. "Just that Bryan was a tool, and he was gunning for Dr. Clowper, and no one is really sad about him being dead."

"Alice Marie Anders," Bree chided, "that's a little harsh, don't you think?"

"Mr. Harper asked what people were saying, and that's what they're saying," Alice said. "It's not my fault people didn't like Bryan. He was a hard-ass."

"Language," Bree warned.

"Really? You're going to complain about my language?"

Finn and Kyle both sputtered with laughter, but Bree just rolled her eyes.

"He was a jerk," Alice insisted. "He spent all of his classes talking about the novels he was supposedly writing and how brilliant he was and how the faculty at Dickerson were totally overrated, never talked about the class readings at all, and then asked these crazy-hard questions. I don't know anyone who got better than a C+ from him."

We all looked at Emily for confirmation. She shrugged. "His teaching skills were not the best," she said. "I told Dr. Landry that he shouldn't put Bryan in the classroom, but we are incredibly short staffed. With more students coming to Dickerson and more required literature and writing requirements, the number of students the department is supposed to teach has doubled over the last twenty years, but the size of our faculty has stayed exactly the same. Landry loves his research, so he's not about to increase the number of classes we each have to teach. As a result, he'll put anyone with a pulse in front of a classroom."

"Who's this Landry person?" Finn asked.

"Jonas Landry. The department chair."

"That reminds me," Alice said. "I stopped by your office and picked up your grant proposal materials." She pulled her keys out of her knapsack, and found a little white rectangle, about the size of a pack of gum, on the ring. "I downloaded it onto my flash drive," she said.

"What is that thing?" I asked.

Everyone except Bree laughed, and I felt like an idiot.

"This is a flash drive," Alice explained. "It's like a little computer disk. Dr. Clowper, if you want to let me use your laptop, I'll copy the file onto your desktop."

"Sure," Emily said, handing over her bag.

Alice pulled out Emily's laptop and powered it up. "I found all the files you asked for—the budget justification, the research proposal—except the budget spreadsheet."

Emily winced. "I probably saved that on the university network drive instead of my hard drive, and that drive is password protected. Stupid."

"Well," Alice continued, "I couldn't find the electronic version of the budget, but I did find a printout in your top desk drawer, right where you said it would be." She tugged a bright blue file folder out of her messenger bag and handed it across the table to Emily.

"Thanks, Alice. The deadline for the application is next week, and I don't want to have to start from scratch. I can recreate the spreadsheet on my home computer, as long as I have the printout. I hope it wasn't too much trouble."

"Nope," Alice said. She laughed. "Though I had to do some fast talking when Dr. Landry and Dr. Gunderson caught me in your office. Gunderson about flipped his lid, but Landry calmed him down. Gunderson's such a fuss-budget."

Emily grimaced. "Sorry about that. But I promise they're both harmless."

"They're the other two members of Bryan's exam committee, right?" Finn asked. "What did they think of Bryan's allegations?"

Emily took a sip of her water. "To be honest, I'm not really comfortable talking about that matter. I haven't spoken yet with the Provost or University counsel or my representative from the faculty senate, but even if the complaint against me is moot, I shouldn't talk about Bryan."

Finn reached across the table and rested a hand on her forearm. "Everyone here is on your side, Em. You can trust us." He gave her arm a gentle squeeze. "I already told you this is off the record," he added with a crooked smile.

Emily returned his smile, and I saw again that flash of warmth and intelligence in her eyes, the one I knew Finn saw when he looked at her.

Suddenly restless, I pushed away from the table, gesturing at Bree's can to see if she wanted another. She shook her head, but I went to get one for myself.

"It's not about trust," Emily explained. "I really cannot comment on a student's academic progress. There's a federal law called FERPA—the Family Educational Rights and Privacy Act—that prevents it. As long as the student's over eighteen, we can't even talk to our students' parents about their grades."

"What about when the student is over eighteen, but dead?" Bree asked, her tone arid.

Emily narrowed her eyes as she met Bree's quizzical expression. "I honestly don't know. That's why I need to speak with the administration before I comment on Bryan's status in the graduate program."

"But you can talk about what a crappy teacher he was, huh?"

"His skills in the classroom had nothing to do with his progress toward his degree."

Either Emily didn't want us to know about her conflict with Bryan, or she was even more of a stickler for the rules than I was. Frankly, I was a little skeptical that the boy would go to such extremes over a single failing grade unless there was some truth to his allegations. In any event, she wasn't going to talk about her beef with Bryan or his beef with her.

Alice finished working her magic with Emily's laptop, handed the bag back, and dropped her keys—with their magical little computer disk—into her own satchel.

"What have you heard, Finn?" I asked. "Any details about what happened that day?"

Finn sighed. "Once again, Mike Carberry got the assignment." Mike had seniority at the *Dalliance Newsletter*, and he went out drinking with half the police force. He tended to land all the big crime stories. "This time, it really makes sense, since we'll want access to the victim's family, and Cal McCormack is not my biggest fan." Finn quirked an eyebrow in a silent salute to me.

Cal and Finn had been barely civil to one another since eighth grade. We'd all been in the same class, and back then

Dalliance High was pretty small. Finn didn't have much patience for Cal's adherence to the rules, and when Cal tattled on Finn for smuggling a pint bottle of rum into a school dance, his disdain turned to full-blown animosity. Meanwhile, Cal had always been protective of me, playing big brother even though we were of an age, and he made no secret that he didn't approve of Finn's rebellious ways. He worried that Finn would break my heart. Even though I was the one who dumped Finn in the end, Cal publicly laid the blame at Finn's feet.

We were all grown-ups, now, but that history lingered just below the surface.

"Thankfully," Finn continued, "Mike's a talkative guy. The cops are still piecing together a timeline, but it looks like Bryan was killed about an hour before he was found, somewhere in the neighborhood of eleven thirty a.m."

"An hour?" I asked. "He was in that office for a whole hour without anyone finding him?"

Emily chimed in. "Most of the faculty and grad student offices are on the next hall over. We don't have any reason to walk past the main office, much less go inside. And since it was a Saturday, none of the administrative staff—the receptionist, the office manager, the advisers—were working."

"So what was Bryan doing in the office?" Bree asked.

"He was supposed to print off the program for the presentations and awards ceremony and then make copies before the formal program started at one o'clock," Alice volunteered.

"He was supposed to do that on Friday," Emily grumbled.

Alice nodded. "But he didn't. Reggie told me he saw Bryan at around ten forty-five. Reggie had just arrived at Sinclair Hall and was on his way back to his office to enter some paper grades before the Honor's Day program, and Bryan was heading to the front office to make the copies."

Alice paused to dig through her backpack again, and pulled out a legal pad. She popped the cap off a ballpoint and began writing a list.

"So Reggie arrived at Sinclair at ten forty-five, and he saw Bryan in the hallway, heading to the front office." She skipped a couple of lines and made a tick mark in the margin of the pad. "Around eleven thirty a.m., someone kills Bryan in the front office." Another tick. "Bryan's body is discovered at twelve twenty-eight p.m."

Bree and I exchanged a look of concern. Alice had taken herself out of the story entirely, reducing the account to a clinical statement of times and events. At some point, she was going to have to come to grips with what she'd seen that day. But it was neither the time nor the place to push her.

Kyle, who'd been watching us from the periphery, spoke up. "What about the blood?"

"What do you mean?" Alice asked.

"Well, I heard this guy got his head bashed in with something heavy—"

"A heavy-duty stapler," Finn offered. "One of those big ones that can staple a hundred pages together."

"Right," Kyle continued. "Someone beat him to death with a heavy metal object, so they must have had blood all over them, right? Whoever it was, it couldn't have been someone who was at that big party. You all would have seen the blood."

I thought the boy made an excellent point, but Emily shook her head.

"That probably rules out most of the guests, but all of us who work in Sinclair Hall, well, we basically live there. Between workout clothes and spare outfits for after all-nighters or for emergencies, like covering someone's class, we all have clothes in our offices."

"Still," Alice said, smiling brightly at Kyle, causing Kyle's cheeks to blaze, "that means whoever killed Bryan either worked in Sinclair Hall or wasn't at the Honor's Day events. That rules out a bunch of people right there. We just have to nail down who had the opportunity and the motive to kill Bryan."

"Alice," I said, "on Saturday, when Emily asked you where Bryan was, you said someone told you he was still running off the programs."

"Reggie," Alice confirmed with a nod.

It seemed to me that this Reggie guy had an awful lot of information about Bryan's whereabouts on the morning of his death. "How did Reggie know that's what Bryan was doing if they hadn't seen each other since ten forty-five?"

Alice frowned. "I think Reggie just assumed that's where Bryan was. Reggie came down to the atrium at about twelve fifteen, and he looked frazzled. I asked him what was wrong. At first he just waved off the question, and then he said Dr. Clowper was going to be pissed off." Alice looked at Emily. "Sorry," she said.

Emily shrugged.

"Anyway, he said he'd seen Bryan that morning and he still wasn't done with the programs. Reggie'd offered to help him with the folding—they share an office, and it wouldn't take Reggie long to enter his grades in his spreadsheet—but Bryan never came back to their office. Reggie said it was typical Bryan to leave you waiting for hours, and Bryan had probably found some hot undergrad to help him with the programs, so Reggie finally gave up and came down to the reception at twelve fifteen."

I wondered why Reggie hadn't checked the department office for Bryan. Maybe he just didn't care whether Bryan got in more hot water with Emily Clowper over the unfinished programs. Or maybe he had looked for Bryan. Maybe he was frazzled because he'd found Bryan's body. Or even because he'd killed him. Something there just wasn't adding up.

Bree had gotten hung up on another part of Alice's story. "Hot undergrad? Why a 'hot' undergrad?"

Alice rolled her eyes. "Everyone knows Bryan had a thing for pretty girls. He was always chatting them up in class and promising them extra credit if they'd help him with filing and stuff in his office. Totally creepy. I mean he's their teacher, you know? That's just weird."

Some raw emotion flashed across Emily's face, and her lips parted as though she were going to interject. But she relaxed and her expression returned to a stoic mask before I could decipher the reaction. Anger? Outrage? Jealousy?

My first instinct was to call her on it. Her relationship with Bryan Campbell was the nine hundred-pound gorilla in the room, and I wanted to confront it. I had to think at least a little of their mutual animosity fell outside the reach of that federal privacy law. But before I could formulate a question that might actually get her talking, Finn tapped the corner of Alice's legal pad.

"Ten forty-five to twelve thirty," he said. "That's a lot of time for Bryan to be MIA in a building crawling with people. Even if faculty didn't regularly pop into the front office, surely someone—a custodian, a student, a parent or guest—someone saw something."

"The question is what did they see," Bree said.

"No," Emily responded. "The real question is why haven't they come forward."

Five

They laid Bryan Campbell to rest just a week after he died, on a dreary Saturday afternoon. I took Alice to the funeral at the Jessamine Street United Methodist Church. She said she wanted to be there to support her Dickerson classmates, but I suspected she planned to report back to Emily.

I went to support Cal.

Cal's sister, Marla Campbell, stood in the vestibule of the church. The League of Methodist Ladies stood in a tight knot around her, propping her up beneath the weight of burying her son.

Marla took after Cal, tall and rawboned with eyes the scorching blue of a gas flame, but a more delicate chin and hair the color of butterscotch candy transformed Cal's stark masculinity into fashion-model beauty. That afternoon, tears streaked her striking face, and a veil of grief dulled her eyes. All the women were dressed in unrelieved black, save Marla, who wore a corsage of crimson and gold—school colors for both the Dalliance High Wildcatters and the Dickerson Dust Devils—on the lapel of her prim black suit.

I ached for the woman, but we'd never been close, and I hated to intrude on the intimacy of her pain. Instead, while Alice wandered off to find her classmates and teachers, I searched out Cal McCormack.

I found him inside the nave of the church. His arrow-straight posture, the hands braced at the small of his back, betrayed his military background as he stood a solitary vigil over the coffin of his nephew.

The lid of the polished oak coffin was closed, covered by a spray of crimson and yellow roses. On a nearby crimson-draped table, a hinged picture frame held two photos: one of a smiling young man, with Cal's angular jaw and Marla's burnished hair, in graduation regalia, the other of the same boy, much younger, wearing a crimson jersey with a gold "44" on his chest and hoisting a bat on his shoulder. A mortarboard and academic hood—black velvet edged with gold—were displayed on the table, along with a baseball bat and glove, and a sash covered with Boy Scout merit badges.

Cal's gaze stayed fixed on the coffin as I approached, but I knew he knew I was there.

I walked right up to him and rested my hand on his arm. I felt the heat and hardness of his bicep beneath the summer-weight wool of his suit coat, felt his muscle tense and then gentle beneath my touch. I just wanted him to know I was there.

"How are you doing, Cal?"

"How do you think I'm doing?" A muscle in his jaw twitched. "I've never felt so useless in my life. My sister's dying out there, and I can't even tell her how her son spent his last hours on this earth."

I frowned. "What do you mean? Bryan was helping get ready for the Honor's Day events, running off the programs for the awards and research presentations."

He shook his head once, a tight, frustrated gesture. "The original was in the copier, but there weren't any copies."

I did a little mental math. "But if that other graduate student, Reggie, saw him heading to make the copies at ten forty-five, what was he doing during that last forty-five minutes?"

That got Cal's full attention. He turned to face me and glared down his nose at me. "Dammit, Tally. How the holy heck do you know all that? Are you meddling in police business again?"

He was talking, of course, about my amateur investigation into the murder of my ex-husband's new fancy-pants girlfriend. A murder for which I was dang near arrested.

I had to crane my neck to look him square in the eye, but I managed it. "First, I wasn't meddling last year, I was trying to save my own bacon, thank you very much. Second, I don't have anything to do with the investigation into Bryan's murder."

"Really," Cal scoffed.

"Really. It's just Alice knows everyone involved, and we were talking about the murder. That's all. Talking, not meddling."

"Were you talking about it with Emily Clowper?"

I winced. "She has been coming by the A-la-mode," I admitted.

"Stay away from that woman, Tally. She's trouble, I promise you."

"I'm not inviting her over for girl talk," I said. "She's Alice's teacher. And Finn's friend."

"Finn? What, are you two going steady again? Or is he paired up with that Clowper woman?"

I flinched at the acid in his voice.

He sighed and shook his head, shaking off his anger the way a hound shakes off rainwater.

"Look, I know he was your high school crush. I get it. But we're not kids anymore, Tally. We have to take responsibility for our actions, be held accountable." He lifted his chin a notch. "If that woman had anything to do with Bryan's death, I will hold her accountable. And you and Finn and Alice better stay the hell out of my way."

The funeral went about like you'd expect.

Cal delivered a typically restrained eulogy with heartbreaking dignity. When he mentioned his sister Marla, and how she'd never be a grandma, one girl—head buried in her arms so that only her blonde ponytail showed above the painfully childish pink and purple scrunchy that fastened it—sobbed so loudly the service paused for her to collect herself.

George Gunderson, one of Bryan's advisers whom I recognized from the group of black-frocked scholars on the day Bryan died, offered a tepid endorsement of Bryan's scholarship and his dedicated service to the university. Marla collapsed in her husband Steve's arms twice. And a parade of fresh-scrubbed young people stood up to say good-bye to their friend, mentioning concerts and baseball games and trips to Austin and New Orleans and Cancun.

I didn't even know the boy, and I was weeping by the time it was over. We all spilled from the gloom of the church into the gray of the overcast late-spring day like accident victims, dazed and directionless.

Thankfully, I caught sight of Deena Silver and made a beeline toward her, taking her hand like a lifeline.

Deena Silver owned the Silver Spoon, Dalliance's most popular catering company. We'd worked together on my ex-husband's company picnic the autumn before, and we'd ended up good friends.

In a plain vanilla world, Deena was cherries jubilee: colorful, flamboyant, sweet and fiery. The day of Bryan's funeral, she wore her lacquered auburn curls pinned high on her crown, and, in honor of the somber occasion, a modest cocoa jersey duster covered her pumpkin and saffron print ankle-length dress.

"I can't believe my Crystal is burying yet another classmate," Deena clucked. A frown tugged at her lush caramel-tinted lips, as she studied her daughter, Crystal Tompkins, across the crowd. Crystal stood beneath a live oak, wrapped in the arms of a slightly pudgy baby-faced young man with a blond crew cut and round, wire-rimmed glasses. "It's been less than a year since Brittanie Brinkman's murder, and now this."

"Were Crystal and Bryan close?" I asked.

Deena shook her head. "No. Bryan was a couple years older than Crystal, a year ahead of Jason." I guessed that Jason was the scholarly blond boy, Crystal's fiancé and a law student at Texas Tech. "But they were all on the debate team together at Dalliance High. Bryan was the team captain the year they won the state championship."

"He must have been brilliant."

"Meh," Deena replied, waggling her hand in a sort of "wishy-washy" gesture.

"Come on," I insisted. "Leading little Dalliance High School to the state championship in debate, working on a Ph.D; he had to have something going on upstairs."

"He was smart enough," Deena conceded, "but he never struck me as brilliant. Maybe it was just because he worked so hard to act smart, that I assumed he wasn't. He talked a big game about going to an Ivy League school and writing the great American novel, then selling the story to Hollywood. But he never seemed to find his way out of Dalliance. Crystal said he could have done whatever he wanted, but that he enjoyed being the big fish in a small pond. I figured he was all sizzle, no steak. Know what I mean?"

I certainly did. In my experience, the people who talked the biggest game were rarely the real players.

"Speaking of steak," Deena continued, "I know this isn't the most appropriate time, but I have a favor to ask."

"Shoot."

"Crystal's been having fits over the groom's cake. She and

Jason have been to a dozen weddings this year, and each bride has outdone the last with a creative twist on the groom's cake. One had a cake shaped like a beer cooler, complete with real beer cans and sugar ice cubes."

"Wow."

"I know. I saw the pictures, and I was quite impressed. But this has really put a lot of pressure on Crystal to surprise Jason with something different, something clever and new. And that's where you come in."

"Whoa," I said. "I don't bake. I mean, I bake for my family, but I don't do fancy cakes and stuff."

"Oh, that's okay," Deena said. "Actual cake isn't necessary anymore. Crystal says she's seen so-called groom's cakes made of cheesecake, pancakes, and the last wedding they went to actually had a groom's steak; a huge slab of beef that the bride presented to her new husband grill-side."

"Really?"

Deena smiled. "Pretty clever, huh? So we were wondering if you could blend up a 'groom's shake.' A signature concoction just for Jason."

Intriguing.

"We're having the wedding at the ranch." Deena's husband, Tom Silver, bred quarter horses on a thriving ranch, the Silver Jack. "We were planning to serve cocktails between the wedding and the reception, while the wedding party is doing pictures. But now we're thinking of serving the groom's shakes then, maybe even in champagne flutes. What do you think?"

I didn't really relish the idea of taking on another commitment for the summer, but Deena had proven a good friend, and it was about time I paid her back for her support.

"I think we can work something out," I said. "Have Crystal give me a call, and she can tell me all about Jason. That way I can pull together a flavor that is both tasty and meaningful."

Deena and I were culinary kin. We both understood the deep emotional connection people have with food, how it can do more than satisfy our physical hunger. She nodded and gave me a discreet high five.

At that moment, Alice approached us, an awkward young man in a rumpled navy suit trailing behind her. I guessed that if he stood up straight he'd be a good head taller than Alice, maybe six one. A shock of ginger curls haloed a long face, with soft, expressive features. The straight slash of his eyebrows and rectangular tortoiseshell glasses framed heavy-lidded blue eyes.

"Hey, Miz Silver," Alice said. "Aunt Tally, this is Reggie Hawking. He'll be teaching that class I was telling you about."

Ah. So this was the boy who had captured Alice's fancy. I didn't see the appeal, personally, but I wasn't a seventeen-year-old girl with a brain the size of Dallas.

Reggie thrust his hand out to shake, but his eyes skittered about, as though he needed something to hold his attention. And we weren't it.

"Alice has told us all about you, Reggie. It's good to finally meet you," I said.

"Me too," he replied, leaving me to wonder whether he was happy to make his own acquaintance or whether he suffered from a polite form of Tourette's syndrome.

"Alice, honey," I said, "are you ready to get going? I should really get back to the store to give your mama a break."

"Sure. Let me just go give my regrets to Professor Gunderson."

She dashed off, leaving Reggie with me and Deena.

"I'm sorry about your friend," I said.

"What?" Reggie shrugged, jerking like a marionette on a string. "You mean Bryan? We were colleagues."

Colleagues. Apparently distinct from friends.

Deena and I exchanged a glance, and I saw a smile flirting

with the corners of her mouth.

Perhaps he simply didn't care what we thought of him, but Reggie didn't let Deena's amusement or my shock slow him down. "Lately, I hardly even saw him."

"I thought you shared an office?" I said.

He nodded. "Yes, but he hasn't been around much this semester. Since the whole blowout with Dr. Clowper his status in the program has been a little uncertain. The university assigned him to work in the research office with Dr. Gunderson."

"The one who gave the eulogy?" Deena asked.

"Yep."

"I thought he was in your department, an English professor."

"He is. But he's also the Vice President for Research Support. They administer all the external funding the faculty and departments receive. The grants, you know."

I could practically feel my eyes glazing over. Where the heck was Alice?

"Sounds interesting," Deena deadpanned.

Reggie shrugged again. "Not really. It's just counting someone else's money, like being a banker. I mean, there's hardly any grant money for the humanities. All the big money's in the natural sciences and information technology."

"Hmmmm," I murmured. That explained why Emily was worried about getting a grant to fund her trip to the East Coast. But, honestly, I found it tough to muster up a lot of interest in the finer points of academic politics. I searched the crowd for Alice.

I caught a glimpse of her standing with a group of somber adults, her penny-bright hair like a flame in their midst. Dr. Gunderson stood next to a tiny woman with snow-white hair and softly rounded features. Another man stood next to

Gunderson, much shorter but with an athletic vitality to his trim form. He nodded earnestly over something Alice said, his narrow bald head tipped down to better hear her. At his side, a woman with a black pantsuit and a bored look on her face stifled a yawn.

"I don't know why Bryan wanted to work over there," Reggie continued, oblivious to our disinterest.

"Money?" Deena suggested. "You know, the promise of a paycheck at the end of the month?"

"I guess. But if you're motivated by money, getting a Ph.D. in English isn't the way to go."

"No?"

"No way. Academic jobs don't pay well, especially in the humanities."

Deena pulled a face. "I got the impression that Bryan planned to use his academic career to pay the bills until he got a big movie deal."

Reggie's lip curled in disgust. "Really? That's depressing. Well, there's nothing glamorous or high-paying about the work Bryan was doing in the grants office, and the few times I did see him this term, he seemed pretty excited about his work with Gunderson. Wouldn't shut up about it. There was something other than money that lit his fire."

"Maybe he was just putting on a brave face," I suggested. "You know, making lemons into lemonade."

Blessedly, Alice popped back into view at that moment.

"All set, Aunt Tally. We can go."

A sigh of relief escaped before I could check myself.

Deena chuckled softly. "It was good to see you Alice. We'll have to have another's girls' day out before my Crystal turns into an old married woman."

Alice blushed and glanced at Reggie, but he was busy digging in his pockets for something.

"See you on Monday, Reggie," she said, a thread of girlish hope in her voice.

"Yep," he responded. "Later." He walked away, listing to one side as he continued to pat himself down.

"What did you think of Reggie?" Alice asked as we made our way through the crowded parking lot.

"Alice, baby," I said as I unlocked the passenger door of my big ol' GMC van, "I've got my fingers crossed that you've got better taste in men than your mama and me."

After meeting, Reggie, though, I was afraid poor Alice had inherited the family curse: a penchant for males who didn't make good mates.

Six

Monday morning, Alice and Bree decided to spend some quality mother-daughter time opening the A-la-mode. More precisely, Bree wanted a chance to pry into her daughter's romantic interest in Reggie Hawking and Alice didn't get a say in the matter.

Either way, it meant I got to enjoy a few moments of peace at the house. Alice, Bree, and I all live in a crumbling Arts and Crafts bungalow in Dalliance's historic district, just a few blocks from the downtown courthouse square. The house is technically mine, a huge chunk of my divorce settlement from my husband of seventeen years, Wayne Jones. But Alice and Bree are family, they make it a home.

That day, I decided to savor the downtime before my hellishly busy summer got into full swing. I camped on the living room sofa, snuggled beneath a patchwork quilt my Grandma Peachy made me when I was five, and watched an '80s romantic comedy on cable. My adolescent orange tabby, Sherbet, perched on the couch cushion behind me, purring loudly and occasionally chewing on my hair.

I nearly jumped out of my skin when the doorbell rang. Sherbet simply yawned and stretched out a paw.

"Who's that, Sherbet?" I slid out from under the quilt, grateful that I'd bothered to change from pajamas into sweats, and shuffled my sock-clad feet across the hardwood to the front door. I peeked out the sidelight window.

Finn Harper stood on my doorstep, dark hair and white oxford both deliciously rumpled, a foil covered pan in his hands. He spotted me, smiled his crooked smile, and gave me a little wave.

I grabbed Sherbet off the couch and draped him over my shoulder so he wouldn't bolt, and then pulled open the wide wooden door. "Finn."

"Morning, Tally." He held up the pan. "I brought banana cake. With cream cheese frosting."

Finn's a wiz in the kitchen, at least when it comes to baked goods. I kid you not, he looks like a movie star and bakes like a pastry chef.

I snatched the pan out of his hands, and stood aside so he could come in. With Sherbet over my shoulder, I led the way to the kitchen. "Watch out for the crap on the floor," I warned.

"Are you folks moving?" Finn asked.

"Ha ha ha. No, Grandma Peachy finally gave up the farm and moved into one of those assisted living places, so we've just inherited another houseful of stuff." I pointed to a heap of plastic shopping bags mounded against the kitchen island. "Like thirty-five years of unfinished craft projects. And we're working a million hours a week, so none of us has had the energy to start sorting and pitching."

"Ah. Is Peachy okay? Did something happen?"

Finn had moved home the year before after his widowed mother had her second stroke. As her only surviving child, he had shouldered the responsibility for her care. She'd been in a holding pattern for nearly a year, not getting worse, but not really improving. I knew it bothered him more than he let on.

"No," I assured him. "Peachy's healthy as a horse and ornery as a fried toad. She just got tired of feeding the animals and rattling around in that house by herself. At the home, she's got people she can torment."

Finn laughed.

I dropped Sherbet next to his kibble, washed my hands, poured us mugs of still-warm coffee, and sliced the banana cake. The cake had a dense, moist crumb, yellow flecked with black, and the scents of vanilla, cinnamon, and nutmeg made my mouth water. Technically, it was a little early in the day for cake. But it would have been rude not to have a slice, right?

Finn shifted stacks of Grandma Peachy's old bank statements aside so we could sit at the kitchen table.

"I know better than to look a gift cake in the mouth, but I have to think you're here for a reason."

Finn looked up at me through his sinfully long lashes as he tucked into his cake. "Guilty," he mumbled around a mouthful of silky cream cheese frosting. He swallowed, took a sip of his coffee, and then got down to business.

"I want to talk to you about Emily. What do you think of her?"

I think she's got more cool in her little finger than I have in my whole, pudgy body. I think she's led a more exciting life than I have and is ten times smarter. I think I'm wildly envious of her, and I also think that I don't trust her even a tiny bit.

"She's nice," I offered. Sherbet leapt up onto the table, and I shooed him off before he could get his teeth into my cake.

"Nice? Em?" Finn laughed. "Emily Clowper is many things, but she sure as heck isn't nice. In fact, she's quite a pill."

"But you like her," I insisted.

"Sure. She's smart and honest and passionate." I felt the heat rising in my face, and Finn chuckled. "I mean she lives with a sort of intensity. Like everything she does, she does it with her whole self. She's just real."

"Oh."

Finn's lips twisted in a rueful smile. "In that sense, she

reminds me of you."

"Oh?" I couldn't imagine someone seeing a common thread between me and Dr. Emily Clowper.

"Yeah. But I'm getting a weird vibe from her now." Finn took a turn at batting away Sherbet. "She's jumpy and more moody than usual and there's this restless energy to her, like she wants to do something or say something and is trying to physically hold herself back."

"Like she's got a secret?" I offered.

"Exactly. Maybe she's just freaked out."

"She has a right to be," I said. "It sounds like her job's in jeopardy, and whether she liked Bryan or not, she worked closely with him. He died violently and she saw the aftermath. I know it's been eating away at Alice, and I have to think Emily is equally distraught."

"Mmm-hmmm."

"But you think it's something more," I said.

He nodded somberly. Silence stretched between us, and we both watched Sherbet turn his attention away from our cake and begin to rummage through the grocery bags full of Peachy's old craft supplies. After rooting his nose around in a half-dozen bags, he emerged triumphant with the tangled remains of a skein of green yarn.

He dropped the yarn on the floor, crouched down low, and pounced on it. Soon he captured a good-sized knot between his front paws and buried his back legs deep in the snarl of wool, kicking frantically, trying to disembowel his imaginary prey.

"I can't even imagine what she's hiding, though," Finn finally said. "I realize you don't know Em as well as I do, but I wanted to see what kind of read you're getting from her."

"Why me? I'm not exactly the best judge of character. I mean, I spent seventeen years married to Wayne Jones while he was running around like an ill-mannered alley cat, and I didn't have a clue."

Finn smiled. "I still trust you, Tally. Right now I trust you more than I trust myself. Emily and I haven't been romantically involved in years and years, but we parted on good terms. I still consider her a friend, and I might be biased."

And I wasn't? Really? Did he really think I could look at Emily Clowper, Finn's ex, without green-tinted glasses? Or that her relationship with my niece didn't set my teeth on edge?

"I don't know, Finn."

"Come on, Tally. Give it to me straight."

As I marshaled my thoughts, I watched the cat. He paused, mid-freak-out, and looked up at me with bloodlust in his eyes, his needlelike fangs showing beneath his velvety whiskers. My sweet kitten would gladly rip a bunny in two if given the chance. Bottom line, we're all just animals, slave to our instincts: to protect our children, to protect ourselves, and sometimes to kill.

"There's something hinky about her," I finally said. "I know you think she couldn't possibly have sexually harassed Bryan, but I get the sense she's hiding something. And I just can't imagine a guy making allegations like that—publicly—and going to the extent of hiring a lawyer just because a teacher failed him on a test."

Finn sipped his coffee. "I've done a little digging about the whole thing with Bryan." He shrugged sheepishly. "I know it's not very loyal to snoop behind her back, but Emily really is legally precluded from talking about the situation."

"Well? Don't keep me in suspense."

"Apparently there are two phases to getting a Ph.D. First, you take classes. Then, after two or three years of courses, you take a comprehensive exam. Which is exactly what it sounds like: you answer questions to demonstrate your mastery of your field. At Dickerson, your committee—the three professors who will oversee the writing of your dissertation—grade your exam.

You need to get them all to pass you on this exam so you can move on and write your dissertation and, eventually, graduate."

"And that's what Bryan failed?"

"Exactly. Bryan's committee included Jonas Landry—"

"The department chair?"

"Yep. It was Jonas Landry, George Gunderson, and Emily. I don't know how Landry and Gunderson voted, but Emily failed Bryan. It was the second time Bryan had taken the test. If you fail twice, you get thrown out of the graduate program."

I whistled. "Wow. This was a big deal."

"Very. The school let Bryan stick around until his complaint against Emily was resolved, but he was living on borrowed time." Finn winced. "Okay, poor choice of words. But you know what I mean. He was about to get the boot from the school."

I broke off a corner of my cake with my fingers and popped it into my mouth, chewed contemplatively, and then licked the frosting from my fingertips. "Given what was at stake, I guess Bryan did have a motive to lie about Emily. Of course, he might have had a motive to lie and still have been telling the truth."

"I just can't see it," Finn insisted.

I held up a hand. "Let's assume Bryan was lying about Emily coming on to him. That still put her job in danger. That still gave her a motive to kill him. Even more of a motive if he was lying, because he was persecuting an innocent woman."

"Oh, come on. You've met her. Can you even fathom her beating some guy's head in with a stapler?"

I had to admit, it was hard to picture Emily doing something so messy. But whether Finn could see it or not, there was a quiet rage simmering just beneath that woman's placid exterior. I looked at my cat, continuing to wage primal war on his yarn. I could absolutely imagine Emily doing whatever it took to protect her livelihood and her life from a malicious liar.

"Look, you asked my opinion, and I gave it to you. I think

just about anyone could commit murder if pushed hard enough."

"Fair enough," Finn said. "But who else was Bryan pushing?"

"Finn, I have no idea. And I'm not really sure I want to know." I took another bite of cake. "At the funeral, Cal accused me of meddling in a murder investigation. I assured him I was doing no such thing. And I meant it. I didn't much enjoy being in the middle of that investigation last year, and I hope to never be in that position again."

Finn smiled, a secret smile that brought to mind all the positions in which I'd found myself last year.

"I get it," he said. "I'll leave you in peace. But can we still meet at the A-la-mode?"

I shot him a glare, but with no real heat behind it. "It's a free country."

He laughed. "Softie. Oh, and..." He paused, a sheepish look on his face. "This may be asking too much, but Emily could really use a distraction from her troubles and she doesn't have many friends here yet."

Yet? The woman had been in Dalliance for almost five years. How could she not have friends yet?

Finn grimaced. "I was thinking it might be good to get her out of the house, so I thought we'd go to karaoke night at the Bar None on Wednesday."

If Emily Clowper sang karaoke, I'd swap suppers with Sherbet.

"You don't need my permission, Finn," I said, embarrassed by the testy tone of my reply.

"I know. But I thought maybe you and Bree would come along." I never thought I'd see the day, but Finn Harper actually blushed a bit. "Underneath that tough-cookie exterior, Emily's an emotional girl. I want to be there for her, but I don't want her to get the wrong impression."

"Jeez, Finn, we're not in high school anymore."

"I know. Maybe it's stupid, but I'd feel better if you came with us."

I sighed. "Oh, all right. Bree will be at karaoke night anyway, and I wouldn't mind a night on the town before we get slammed with summer customers. As long as we go late. I want to get the A-la-mode locked up and Kyle and Alice safely home before I head out."

Tension drained from Finn's body and his slow grin spread across his face. "Deal," he said. "So I'll see you Wednesday?"

"Guess so," I replied, leading him to the front door.

I swung open the door to let Finn out, and found Cal McCormack standing on my front porch, fist poised to knock.

Cal's military background showed in his dress: his dark green shirt was tucked evenly in his jeans, the tail of his belt had been slipped through the loops, and the toes of his boots shone with a fresh coat of polish. But that morning, there were signs of wear in his demeanor. His close-cropped salt-and-pepper hair stuck up all higgledy-piggledy on one side of his head, and dark circles around his cerulean eyes stood out on his drawn face.

"Hey, Cal," Finn drawled, amused.

"Finn." Cal's expression betrayed no emotion at all.

"I'll see you later, Tally," Finn called over his shoulder as he sauntered down the walk.

"Come on in, Cal," I said, stepping out of his way.

He walked in, but stopped awkwardly just inside the door, like he wasn't sure if he was really welcome. Sherbet, always interested in new visitors, came trotting into the front room with his yarn trophy clamped in his tiny jaws. Cal crouched down and scratched the cat behind the ears, then stood and faced me.

"I stopped by the A-la-mode, but Bree said you were at

home this morning." His jaw tightened. "She didn't mention you had company."

"She didn't know," I said.

One dark eyebrow arched.

"No, what I mean is Finn just stopped by. He brought banana cake. You want some?"

Cal looked at me like I'd suggested he might want to streak naked through the courthouse square. "No. Thank you."

"So what can I do for you?"

"I, uh..." He stopped and cleared his throat. "Thanks for coming to the, uh, the church yesterday."

Funeral. I'd never known Cal McCormack to show a lick of fear, but he couldn't say that little word.

"Of course, Cal. I hope you know how sorry I am. For you and for Marla."

"Yeah, well, it means a lot." He studied his boots. "You know, when bad things happen, you know who your friends are. They're the ones who call or drop you a note and say, 'hey, if there's anything I can do, just holler.'"

He paused again, and made a little sound in the back of his throat as though he were agreeing with himself. Then he looked up, and fixed me with the full power of that blistering blue gaze.

"You also learn who's more than a friend. Who's family. They're the ones who walk right up to you and hold out their hands without even waiting for you to ask."

I knew what it cost Cal to stand in the middle of my living room, a marmalade tabby winding between his feet, and let a little of the tenderness inside his hard cowboy heart show. And it did my own heart good to know that the bond we'd formed as children had survived our years of estrangement. I didn't have much family, but what I had I held close. I'd gladly welcome Cal into that circle.

On impulse, I closed the gap between us and wrapped my

arms around him. Cal stood nearly a foot taller than me, and I thought he might have a gun somewhere on his person, so the best I could manage was an awkward hug. I felt him stiffen, but then his own hands fumbled across my back until he held me tight against him.

I never saw a tear in his eyes or felt moisture against my cheek, but in his own way Cal McCormack cried that morning. Ripples of tension passed through his body, as though he were convulsing, heaving the pain from his body, and my hair muffled a raw sound that welled up from deep within him.

We stood that way for a long time, neither of us speaking, just letting the years melt away and feeling the old bonds of deep friendship.

Finally, Cal broke the silence. "Tally?"

"Hmmm?"

"Where's the yarn?"

"What?" I asked, pulling away.

Cal pointed at the ground behind me. "Where's the yarn?"

I turned and looked down at the floor. Sherbet crouched on the carpet, staring, slightly dazed, at the bare floor in front of him.

He belched daintily.

"Oh, crap," I muttered, dropping to my haunches and searching the floor for the yarn. It didn't seem possible that such a small cat, still little more than a kitten, could have consumed a whole ball of yarn in the blink of an eye. But the yarn had been there, and now it wasn't. I lifted the edge of Grandma Peachy's quilt from where I'd left it hanging off the couch, scattered the throw pillows, and knocked over a stack of Alice's schoolbooks. All in vain. The yarn was definitely gone.

Unless we had a ghost, the cat had eaten it. I'd never had a pet of any sort, much less a cat, but common sense told me that eating a yard of string couldn't be good. I scooped up the cat, his body as sleek and firm as an otter in my grasp. "What do I do?" I said, looking frantically at Cal for guidance.

His emergency-response training kicked into gear.

"Where's the cat carrier?" he asked.

"I don't know," I wailed. "The house is such a freakin' mess. I don't know where anything is."

"Calm down, Tally. It's okay. We don't need the carrier." He disappeared down my hallway and returned a moment later with a bath towel. He shook it out and laid it across the back of the couch.

Gently, he pried Sherbet out of my hands, set the cat on the towel, and wrapped him up like a mummy. Just a blue terry-cloth football with a cat head sticking out of the top. Cal tucked the edge of the towel into a fold, so the bundle was secure, and handed the cat back to me.

"Come on, Tally. Let's go. I'm driving."

And just like that, our roles reversed. Strong, silent Cal had taken charge.

Seven

All Creatures Animal Hospital smelled like wet dog and fear. I cradled Sherbet, still cocooned in his periwinkle towel, close to my body while Cal did the admitting paperwork for me.

A vet tech in hot pink scrubs directed us to the plastic chairs that ringed the waiting room and assured us a vet would be with us soon.

I looked down at Sherbet in my lap. He stared up at me with eyes like yellow marbles. I know he's a cat, and I know they have very small brains, but I felt like we connected in that moment. He opened his mouth in a silent meow, and my heart about broke.

"I'm sorry, little man. I know you didn't mean to do anything wrong. And I'm not going to let anything happen to you."

I scratched behind his ears, and a tear escaped my eye to fall on his silky little head.

Cal's big hand reached out and grasped mine, and he rested our twined fingers on Sherbet's back.

"He'll be fine, Tally," Cal whispered.

"He's a pretty cat."

I hadn't even noticed there was another person in the room, so her compliment startled me. The woman had a little kick-dog on her lap, one of those dogs that looks like someone stuck a small fox in a clothes dryer and let it get all puffy. This one had fur the color of ground cinnamon, but with a silvery muzzle and a frosting of white along the edges of his ears.

The woman herself looked like a shopping mall Mrs. Claus: an elfin woman with snow-white curls around peppermint-pink cheeks, a ring of delicate cream lace around the collar of her evergreen-colored blouse. She looked vaguely familiar, and I was pretty sure I'd seen her before. In real life, not just on a Norman Rockwell calendar.

The woman smiled, dimpling cheeks as soft and powdery as unbaked biscuits, and the dog's tongue lolled out in a matching doggy grin. That's when I placed her. She'd been at Bryan's funeral, sitting with the faculty and representatives from Dickerson.

"Is your little friend sick?" the woman asked.

"He ate yarn," I said. A nervous laugh escaped me. "That sounds ridiculous, doesn't it?"

"Oh, no," she said. "I'm a dog person, aren't I Ginger?" The dog on her lap shuffled his tiny feet, the tags around his neck jingling merrily. The woman's voice sounded curiously flat and nasal to me. I couldn't place the accent, maybe something East Coast, but she definitely wasn't a Texan. "But my niece Madeline has a cat. She's had terrible trouble with that cat eating all manner of things—strings, ribbons, dental floss, rubber bands. He's already had surgery six times to remove foreign bodies."

Six times?

I met Sherbet's terrified yellow gaze again. I tried to send him a telepathic message: Let's not make a habit of this, okay?

"What about Ginger, there? Is she okay?" Cal asked. I should have inquired myself, but I was way too freaked out by the thought of my little buddy going under the knife to be polite.

"He," the woman corrected. "Ginger's a boy. We're here all the time, aren't we, Ginger?" She lowered her face and the tiny dog licked the tip of her nose. She giggled girlishly. "Ginger's getting up in years and has all the same problems his mommy has. Arthritis, diabetes, a heart murmur. Though thankfully he didn't get the cancer." She stroked a finger over the dog's delicate throat, and he tipped back his head to give her better access. "I tell George, my husband, that he'll probably have to have both me and Ginger put down at about the same time."

She winked at us. "George is not amused."

Despite my anxiety over Sherbet's tummy, I found myself smiling back at the woman. That little bit of gallows humor showed a strength at odds with her delicate femininity. I pegged her as a tough old bird, and I had a soft spot for tough old birds.

"Detective McCormack, isn't it?" she asked. Cal nodded. "I'm Rosemary Gunderson. My husband is George Gunderson, one of Bryan's professors. I'm so sorry for your loss."

Cal's fingers tightened around mine.

"Thank you," he said gruffly.

Rosemary stared at me expectantly. I didn't feel like making small talk, even with this charming woman, but good manners demanded I introduce myself.

"I'm Tally Jones, and this here's Sherbet," I said, raising the cat a couple inches in greeting.

"Tally Jones, Tally Jones," she muttered. Then her eyes lit up. "Of course, the ice cream lady!"

I laughed in spite of myself.

Rosemary prattled on. "Etta Harper is a dear friend, and she's been urging me to come try your ice cream. Unfortunately, George doesn't care for sweets much. I've been trying to tempt him into a lemon soufflé or a square of tiramisu at the Hickory Tavern every week for two years, and I still have yet to succeed. Their desserts are absolutely heaven. Every now and then he'll order one, but he never even touches it. Either I eat it for breakfast the next morning or he takes it to work to butter up the secretarial staff."

That introduction packed a wealth of information about the Gundersons' position in Dalliance Society. Etta Harper was Finn's mother, and the Harpers had helped found Dalliance. Etta Harper never socialized much with women outside her social stratum, and she'd been housebound for almost a year following a series of strokes. If Rosemary Gunderson still had contact with Mrs. Harper, she was a dear friend, indeed.

A comfortably wealthy dear friend, at that. The Hickory Tavern boasted the most upscale and expensive menu in town. My ex, Wayne, was a successful businessman, but the Hickory Tavern was still a special treat, the sort of place we went for anniversaries and birthdays. Yet the Gundersons dined there every week. Reggie had made it sound like professors lived in poverty, but apparently, being a professor could pay pretty well.

Rosemary looked from my face to Cal's and back again. An impish sparkle in her eyes, she glanced down at our hands, once again clasped together on Sherbet's back.

"I didn't know you two were close," she said.

Cal and I jumped apart like we'd been stung.

I felt the blush licking up my cheeks. I cut my eyes to the side to catch a peek of Cal. To my surprise, his mouth twitched in something like a smile. And I can't say I approved of the mischievous glint in his narrowed eyes.

"No, ma'am. I'm gonna have to get in line behind Tally's other suitors."

"Cal McCormack," I gasped, mortified. "You make it sound like I'm the town tramp."

He smiled for real at that, and a tiny corner of my heart fluttered to see him forget his troubles, even at my expense. "I think you and I have very different ideas about what that word 'tramp' means. I'm just saying you're popular with the fellas these days. Not that you're returning the favor."

"Oh, for crying out loud," I muttered, hugging Sherbet

closer.

Rosemary giggled. "I think this young man is pulling your pigtails, dear."

Cal laughed. "I might be at that."

The vet tech came into the waiting room and called Sherbet's name, saving me from having to respond to Cal's teasing.

I picked up my little bundle and headed back to see the doctor.

"Don't worry," Cal called behind me. "I'll be right here waiting for you."

Eight

Two days later, on the Wednesday after the funeral, I emerged from my bedroom to find Alice waiting for me at the kitchen table, two cups of freshly brewed coffee and toasted bagels already laid out. Beneath the scent of French roast and warm cinnamon, I smelled a con.

"What do you want?" I asked.

"Can't I make you breakfast without it being some scam?" she responded, eyes wide with forced innocence.

"You can make me breakfast, but you don't. And given the events of this past week, I'm a little suspicious of your motives."

Alice reached out to pick up my cup and plate. "Does that mean you don't want it?"

I rapped her gently on the head with my knuckles. "Put that back, kiddo. Even a blackmail bagel is tasty." She smiled as she let my breakfast go.

I slid into my chair, pulled my bagel a little closer, and took a sip of my coffee. "Spill it."

"I made you a date," Alice said.

I did an old-fashioned spit-take.

"You what?"

Alice laughed, a delighted musical sound. She snagged a handful of paper napkins out of the holder—fashioned out of two plaster-of-Paris handprints, Alice's pudgy little toddler fingers splotched with red and yellow paint—and passed them to me.

"Not a real date," she said, as she helped me mop up the drops of coffee. "I e-mailed Reggie Hawking last night to tell him you were interested in coming back to school and wanted to talk to someone about getting into Dickerson as a nontraditional student."

"Nontraditional?"

"Not eighteen," she clarified.

"Well, I'm definitely not eighteen, but I'm also not particularly interested in being a college student right now." And I was crazy-not-interested in spending alone time with Reggie Hawking. Alice might be crushing on the boy, but I found him pompous and self-absorbed.

Sherbet, who had already recovered from his recent yarnectomy, leapt onto the table. His flexible Elizabethan collar, meant to keep him from chewing out his stitches, folded beneath him, and he had to scramble his front paws for traction, but he was highly motivated. He had a sixth sense about possible people-food, and before I could push him back to the floor, he snatched half a buttered bagel and bolted. I sighed. Sherbet had wretched manners, but I didn't know how to socialize him. Besides, after the yarn scare, I didn't have the heart to chase him down and wrestle the bagel away from him. His bald little tummy broke my heart.

"I know you don't want to go to school," Alice said, unfazed by the pilfering feline. "I just need you to keep Reggie occupied for about fifteen, twenty minutes."

I had gone from suspicious to downright distrustful. "Why?"

"Does it matter?"

"Of course it matters."

"Oh, all right. I want to look around in his office a bit."

"For what? Evidence of a girlfriend?" I teased.

She looked flummoxed, but then she laughed. "I guess I'm my mother's daughter after all, huh?" She sighed. "Yeah, I was in his office every day last week, but he's always there, too. He has one of those electronic picture frames, where you can keep lots of digital images, but it's always on a picture of him in a cap and gown. He's a puzzle, you know? An enigma. I just want to flip through the pictures and try to get a better feel for who he is. Look for pictures of his parents, his friends, his pets."

"I don't know, Alice. That's not a very healthy thing to do." Not to mention that it was weird that the only picture on the boy's desk was of himself, alone. That didn't bode well.

"Relax, Aunt Tally. I'm not turning into a stalker. I was, uh, thinking of asking him out, and I don't want to put myself out there if he has a girlfriend."

"Really?"

"Yes." She cleared her throat, nodded once, and said it again more forcefully. "Yes. I think Reggie Hawking is cute and smart and I want to ask him to go to the movies."

She sounded so earnest, like she was planting her flag on virgin ground, and I almost laughed. One small step for Alice, one giant step for girl-kind.

"I still don't think it's a good idea to snoop."

"Really? You did a little snooping last year, didn't you? And I seem to recall helping you with that." She had a point. I hadn't even given her a choice, simply impressed her into service as a diversion so I could chat up Crystal Tompkins about the murder of my ex's girlfriend.

"But how old is this Reggie person?"

"I don't know, exactly. He's finishing his fourth year of grad school, so maybe twenty-five? Twenty-six?

"So, eight or nine years older than you? That's a pretty big age difference."

Alice sighed impatiently. "Aunt Tally, I've spent my whole

life hanging around with people who are older than I am. Jeez, if I'm stuck dating boys my age, I'm stuck with Kyle."

She managed to make it sound like dating Kyle was a fate worse than death. Poor Kyle. He looked at Alice like she hung the moon, and there was a time when she was equally fascinated with him. She was the gilded princess, with porcelain skin and pure heart. He was the tarnished knight, with brooding eyes and a gift for getting into trouble.

Where Alice excelled in school, taking honors classes and graduating early, Kyle had long been labeled a troublemaker and shunted off to remedial classes. He could hold his own when he and Alice sparred, so I had to assume his academic woes were a result of his bad attitude rather than some lack of ability. Still, the two would never have met if Kyle hadn't taken the job at the A-la-mode so he could make restitution for a mailbox smashing spree from the summer before. But once they entered each other's orbit, the peculiar physics of attraction took over and they became locked in a tug-of-war as inevitable as gravity.

Then, something over the past year—either a fight they'd managed to keep private, or simply the shifting circumstances of their lives—had changed that dynamic, leaving it lopsided and sad.

"Besides," Alice added, "I'm going to do it one way or another, even if I have to pick the lock to get in there. So you may as well stop trying to talk me out of it. If you help me, at least I won't get caught."

I took a bite of my bagel and chewed thoughtfully. Baked goods came dear, it seemed.

"Fine," I said. "What do I have to do?"

Dickerson's student union looked like a boutique shopping mall. The Gish-Tunney Center, named for the two alums whose generous bequests funded its construction, housed student organization offices and a ballroom on the third floor; a bookstore, copy center, and elegant meeting rooms on the second floor; a large lounge and small eateries on the main floor; and a state-of-the-art performance space in the basement.

Reggie Hawking leaned down so his mouth was close to my ear. "It's too loud to talk in here. We can get a drink and take it out to the patio."

We'd left Alice back at Sinclair Hall, setting up a grade book for their American Literature class on Reggie's desktop computer. He led the way to the counter of the Jump and Java, a standard-issue espresso bar with a pastry case bursting with baked goods. He ordered a large coffee. "Make that two," he said, glancing at me.

"Make that one," I said, reaching a hand to get the clerk's attention. Whether I wanted coffee or not, it wasn't this kid's place to order for me. "It's hotter than a whore in a church out there. If we're taking this outside, I'll stick with iced tea. And a brownie." To get through even ten minutes with this guy, I needed chocolate to sustain me.

Reggie paused in the act of rummaging in his pocket, met my eyes, and smiled. For the first time since we'd met, I felt like he didn't just look at me, but actually saw me. When all that scattershot boy genius energy focused on me, and his mobile features settled into sensuous lines, I could sort of see why Alice had a crush on him. He was still not my type, but I could at least wrap my brain around his appeal.

"That's a dollar fifty for the coffee and four dollars for the tea and brownie," the clerk said.

I laid four bills on the counter. Reggie picked them up and slipped them in his pocket. "I'll pay for both with my i-Cash," he said.

He pulled a yellow plastic card from his wallet and swiped it across a small black box with a glowing red eye.

"What's that?" I asked.

"It's my student ID," he said. "Students and faculty can put money in an account and use our ID's to pay for stuff at the campus stores. We get a discount when we use them."

Neat. That meant he was paying less than four bucks for my drink and snack, but he sure wasn't handing me back change. Oh, well, I thought, I guess this makes me a patron of the arts.

"We can even use them in the vending machines," he continued. "Of course, some of the wingnuts over in the art department complained that the university is trying to keep tabs on us, tracking us like animals in the wild. But I think it beats the heck out of carrying around change or trying to get a dollar bill flat enough to feed into the machine."

We found a table out on the student union's shaded patio. The damp weekend had evolved into a muggy Monday that likely signaled the beginning of the unrelenting brutal Texas summer. Reggie pursed his lips and blew gently across the surface of his coffee. The thought of drinking hot coffee in the middle of that sauna-like weather made my neck prickle with sweat. I took a big gulp of my sweet tea, relishing the tingle of the crushed ice against my upper lip.

We sat in silence for a few minutes, as I tried to think of something clever to say. A thought popped into my head that it might someday be this awkward to converse with Alice.

"It must be interesting working with all these bright young students every day," I offered.

Reggie shook his head. "College kids are basically sociopaths."

I laughed.

"No, really," Reggie insisted. "My first year in grad school, I had a roommate, a doctoral student over in the psych department. One night after we finished grading a stack of finals, we broke out a bottle of tequila and started bitching about our students. He showed me the definition of a sociopath in one of his textbooks. I don't remember it exactly, but it was something about being completely self-absorbed, lacking empathy, and being willing to lie and cheat to get what you want. Pretty much sums up most college kids."

It seemed like it came reasonably close to summing up most of the adults I knew, too, but I kept that observation to myself. "That's a little harsh, don't you think?"

Now it was Reggie's turn to laugh. "Not harsh, just realistic. I had a kid last year actually lie about his mother dying to get out of a midterm. That's some serious bad karma."

"Sounds like he was desperate," I said.

He shrugged his wild, spastic shrug. "Maybe," he conceded, "but when I called him on it, demanded to see a death certificate or an obituary or something, he just smiled. Like 'Oh, well, I guess you caught me.' No tears, no apologies, nothing."

I broke off a corner of the brownie and popped it into my mouth. "Okay, so he was kind of a sleaze. But that's just one kid. Surely they're not all that bad."

Reggie sipped his coffee, slurping noisily. "That was an extreme case," he admitted, "but I catch them lying all the time about being sick, having their cars broken into, and about halfway through the semester, grandparents start dropping like flies. Some of them are good kids, but they just don't have any perspective, you know?"

Now that was something I understood. It had been less than a year since Brittanie Brinkman died, and I had come to grips with the fact that my ex-husband's chippie girlfriend was more immature than evil. She just lacked perspective.

"Especially these days," Reggie continued. "Kids today have so much structure in their lives: every minute of their day is some scheduled event or activity, they're told exactly what they have to learn for every test, and they all know they're going to college when they graduate high school. At least the kids who end up at Dickerson know they're going to college. They never have to make decisions for themselves, so they never have to make good decisions, you know?"

I fought a smile at the notion of this boy in his mid-twenties complaining about "kids today."

"So that's what you do? Teach them to make good decisions?"

"Me?" Reggie leaned back in his chair. His gaze grew distant, and one corner of his mouth quirked up in something like a smile. "Hardly. At best, I teach them to write." He made some inarticulate sound in the back of his throat.

"So if you don't like teaching, why are you studying to be a professor?"

It seemed like a reasonable question to me, but Reggie snorted.

"I'm not studying to be a professor, I'm studying to be a scholar."

"Oh."

"I wouldn't expect you to understand. Most people don't."

Well, la-di-freakin'-da.

"Most civilians," he said with a small smile, amused at his own joke, "don't realize that college professors teach, but that's only a small part of the job. Most of the job involves doing research in our field, publishing in scholarly journals, and writing books."

To be honest, I didn't understand the world in which Reggie and Emily lived, the world into which Alice was plunging headlong, but I did know that I had no patience for this sort of pompous BS. I was itching to show this kid that I wasn't a total bumpkin.

"It must be tough to do all that without grant money," I said, and smothered my smile of triumph over the look of surprise on his face.

"How did you?"

"I guess I pay attention pretty well for a civilian," I said. "You said at Bryan's funeral that there wasn't much grant money for the humanities."

"Oh, right. I guess I did."

I glanced at my watch. I'd promised Alice I'd keep Reggie out of Sinclair Hall for twenty minutes, but time was dragging. I needed to keep him talking. Alice had suggested asking questions about being a nontraditional student, but I hadn't prepared any questions and none were coming to mind. In the end, it didn't matter what we talked about, as long as I kept him occupied a bit longer. So I decided to keep him on the subject of grant money.

"So if there isn't any grant money for the humanities, why does Professor Gunderson run that office?"

"I have no idea," Reggie said with a shrug. "At first, he got assigned to the office as an interim director, because the last guy left without any notice. He wailed about what a sacrifice he was making for the university, but then a month later he actually applied for the position on a permanent basis. No one else wanted to deal with the bureaucratic headaches, so he got the position."

"And took Bryan with him," I mused.

"Oh, no," Reggie said. "Bryan only started working there this spring, after he failed his comps. Bryan couldn't teach when his status in the department was up in the air. Of course, he wanted to go back to doing research with Dr. Landry, because Landry's about to hit the big time with his new book. But even though Bryan worked for Landry last summer and was already familiar with Landry's work, Landry said no."

"Why?"

Reggie shrugged. "The official story was that it wouldn't be appropriate for Landry, as chair, to work with a student with a complaint against the department. But that's BS. I think Bryan did a half-assed job last summer, and Landry wanted someone who could pull his weight."

"What makes you think that?"

Reggie smirked. "I heard Landry bitching about Bryan just before fall semester ended. He said something about how Bryan spent too much time on the effing Internet reading effing blogs."

His smirk faded and he looked a little abashed. "It's not like I was eavesdropping or anything."

Which meant, of course, that he had been eavesdropping.

"It's just that Landry was talking on his cell phone as he left Sinclair Hall, and I was sitting outside grading papers. It was right after Thanksgiving, when we had that weird heat wave, remember?" I nodded. "Usually Landry is laid back—trying to be the cool cat, you know?—but he was on a tear that day. I couldn't help but overhear what he was saying."

Reggie took a sip of his coffee. "Anyway, the bottom line is the department didn't know what to do with Bryan, but Dickerson doesn't pay anyone unless they work. Sticking him over in the research office was an easy fix. But I don't think Gunderson particularly liked Bryan either. He just took one for the team, as they say."

Jeez, I thought, despite all the tearful tributes at his funeral, it was looking more and more like Bryan Campbell was utterly friendless. I wondered how one young man with so much promise could have become such a pariah.

"So," Reggie said, snapping my attention back to my more immediate concern, "Alice said you're interested in enrolling in Dickerson."

I raised my glass of iced tea in a mock toast. "You make it sound so appealing. How can I resist?"

Reggie was a lousy ambassador for Dickerson. Once the conversation turned from his own place in the universe and departmental gossip to the life of an undergraduate, he completely checked out. He answered my questions with disinterest bordering on, well, a coma. When I could pry more than a sentence out of him, he showed utter disdain for the students he taught, the ranks of which I ostensibly wished to join.

Eventually, I decided Alice had had plenty of time to check through Reggie's pictures, and I was feeling less and less good about helping her romance the boy, so I suggested we head back to Sinclair Hall.

As we approached Reggie's office, I heard the rumble of a male voice coming from inside. I stepped up the pace and beat Reggie to the door, only to find Alice sitting in Reggie's seat chatting quietly with Cal McCormack, who was sitting at the other desk in Reggie's office.

"Hey, Tally," he drawled. "I thought you weren't meddling."

"I'm not," I said.

"Huh. Seems you and I are gonna have to break out the ol' dictionary and look up 'meddling.' Because I just caught this little lady going through Bryan's desk."

Nine

That night, before we hit the Bar None, Alice, Emily, and Finn had another strategy-session-slash-gossip-fest at the Remember the A-la-mode.

When we were all gathered around a table—everyone except Kyle, who had camped in a booth with his schoolbooks, pretending to study—I gave my niece the hairy eyeball. "Are you gonna tell your mama what happened, or am I?"

She looked stricken, betrayed.

"Tell me what?" Bree asked.

"It wasn't a big deal, but Aunt Tally went to get a cup of coffee with Reggie so I could have a few minutes alone in Reggie's office."

"And why would you want to be alone in Reggie's office?"

"Because it was also Bryan's office," Alice admitted.

Finn's jaw dropped, and Emily looked completely horrified. Bree, on the other hand, didn't look terribly surprised. Pissed, but not surprised.

"Alice Marie Anders, are you telling me you pawed through a murder victim's personal belongings?"

Alice shrugged. "I didn't get around to the pawing part. Detective McCormack didn't let me."

That was the last straw. Bree slapped her forehead with the palm of her hand. "Hand to God, little girl, you're gonna be the death of me," she moaned.

"Mom, it's okay."

"It's not okay. My daughter's in trouble with the law."

"I'm not in trouble," Alice huffed. "And you're one to talk. Didn't you and Aunt Tally break into Uncle Wayne's office last year? You actually committed a crime."

Bree glared at me, and I raised my shoulders in a helpless shrug. Alice was absolutely right. We were terrible role models.

When I didn't offer support, Bree turned on me. "I can't believe you helped her," she hissed.

I held up my hands. "In my own defense, Alice told me she needed me to keep Reggie occupied so she could snoop around and make sure he didn't have a girlfriend, because she was thinking of asking him out."

"Oh, well, in that case, I guess it's okay," Bree drawled. "If you were just helping her to act like a crazy stalker instead of helping her commit a B&E."

A tiny part of my brain recognized that she had every right to be p.o.'ed at me, but I chafed at having my reckless, party-girl cousin, who had spent a lifetime relying on me to bail her out of messes and marriages, accuse me of irresponsibility. Especially in front of Finn and Emily.

"Hey," I snapped back, "she was threatening to pick the lock to his office door. At least with my help she just entered, without the breaking part."

"Honestly, Tally—"

"Mom! It's not Aunt Tally's fault. I manipulated her."

Without hesitation, Bree refocused her ire back on her child. "You mean you lied to her. Do I need to haul your skinny be-hind back to Sunday School?"

Alice blushed pomegranate pink. "I didn't exactly lie," she said. "I am going to ask Reggie to go to a movie with me. Kyle told me the Dalliance Rec Department is showing the Rocky Horror Picture Show outside, at Lonestar Park, in a couple of weeks."

From my position at the table, I had a good view of Kyle. The boy looked gutshot. If only Alice knew the power she had to squish his heart to smithereens. Emily, too, appeared troubled by Alice's interest in Reggie. I wondered if she shared my concern about the age difference between the couple, or if Emily, as Reggie's teacher and adviser, knew an even better reason Alice should keep her distance.

"See, I didn't lie to Aunt Tally. I just didn't tell her the entire truth. I planned to look through both Reggie's and Bryan's desks."

Now there was no mistaking the panic on Emily's face. Was she upset that Alice would take such a risk? That Alice was too deeply involved in a potentially dangerous situation? Or was she worried about what Alice might find in Bryan's desk?

Bree had plenty of wrath to go around that night. She pointed a purple manicured finger at Emily Clowper. "Did you put her up to this?"

Emily appeared genuinely distraught. "Me? Absolutely not."

Bree didn't look convinced.

"Listen, I gave Alice my office key already, and that key opens all of the offices on the first floor of Sinclair, including Bryan and Reggie's. If I'd put Alice up to this, I would have told her to use the key, and she wouldn't have had to involve Tally at all." Emily laid her hand over her heart as though swearing an oath. "I would never ask Alice to dig through Bryan's things."

"I wish I'd known that thing about the keys," Alice muttered. Then she sighed. "Look, Mom, it was all my idea. Besides, I didn't get to do much digging before Detective McCormack came in."

She lowered her face and looked up at us through her lashes. "But I did find this." She ducked down to search through her bag, and sat up with a cube of paper.

A calendar, one of those page-a-day things.

We all stared at it in amazement, as though she had produced the Holy Grail out of her knapsack. Even Bree's anger faded in the face of this relic from Bryan's desk.

Finally, Finn reached across and picked up the cube of paper and turned it over in his hands. He read the cover. "Three hundred sixty-five days of baseball trivia, an academic year calendar."

Across the room, I saw Kyle perk up. Kyle didn't play sports, but I guess he had a more intellectual interest in baseball.

Alice took the calendar back. "This is what I thought was interesting," she said.

She flipped through the calendar to the page for November 15th of the previous year, then turned the little cube around so we could all see it better. There was a note scrawled in all capital letters: "NO OSTERGARD!!!"

"Who or what is Ostergard?" Bree asked.

"I don't know," Alice conceded. "But it looks like it mattered to Bryan a lot. See?"

She flipped back to November 20: "OSTERGARD?"

Then she flipped forward to November 26: "O— DEFINITELY FAKES."

"Weird," I said.

We all turned to Emily. After all, Bryan moved in her world. "What do you think?" Finn asked.

Emily looked troubled. "I'm not sure. I've never heard of a student named Ostergard. But the name is familiar. It looks like Bryan was quite a baseball fan. Maybe it's a player?"

Kyle piped up. "There was a player in the 1920s named Red Ostergard, but he only played a year. I doubt he's talking about Red Ostergard."

We all stared in stunned silence at Kyle. Who knew the boy had that kind of trivia at his fingertips?

Emily frowned. "I just don't know. It might be significant. It might not."

Alice's face fell.

"No, no," Emily said, reaching out to pat the girl's hand. "I appreciate the effort. And it might actually mean something, I just don't even know where to begin looking for significance."

Alice shrugged and pushed the calendar away, and went to get a soda. Emily and Finn started chatting, and Bree watched their exchange with unconcealed interest.

Kyle picked up the calendar and started paging through the days. I'd never seen the boy so interested in reading. His usually sullen expression took on an intensity that gave his face definition and provided a glimpse of the man he would become.

I was marveling at the thought that our favorite juvenile delinquent would one day—possibly soon—be a grown-up, with real responsibilities, when Kyle frowned. He flipped a page of the calendar, then flipped it back, and again.

"Uh, there's a page missing," he said.

Alice, who had returned to the table with a can of Dr. Pepper, swung her head around to look at him, her expression deeply peeved. "What?" she snapped.

He met her gaze defiantly. "I said," he enunciated with exaggerated care, "there's a page missing."

"I don't think so," Alice snipped. "I started at the very beginning and checked every single day, right up to the murder."

Kyle sniffed, clearly not impressed. "Well, the page that's missing is for after the murder, smarty pants." He rolled his shoulders, as though the mantle of "man with answers" didn't feel comfortable there. "I mean, it's not like that guy knew he was going to die. He had plans."

For a moment, we all just stared at Kyle, stunned at both what he'd said—the unwitting pathos of it—and by the fact that he'd strung so many words together at all. Bless his heart, Kyle was a silent boy. As Grandma Peachy would say, most of the time he wouldn't say shit with a mouthful. Three sentences amounted to a veritable dissertation.

Finn finally reacted, fishing a stumpy yellow pencil from his shirt pocket as he crossed the floor to Kyle's booth. He slid into the seat across from the teen. "Show me," he said.

Kyle sat up a little straighter. "Here." He held open the calendar. "This is where the missing page should be."

Holding the pencil at an angle, so the side of the lead touched the paper instead of the point, he shaded the page below. My by-the-book nature winced at what surely amounted to tampering with evidence. Assuming, of course, there was anything on the page that actually mattered.

Something in Finn's expression changed, and I knew he'd found something.

"I don't know what it means," he grumbled.

"What does it say?" Emily asked.

"It's just letters. 'K-U-S' or 'K-V-S'? Geez, the kid's printing is tough to make out. Maybe that's an 'R' instead of a 'K'? That's the first line, then there's a phone number, and then more letters 'Q-U-I-T-A-M.'"

Bree piped up. "The first letters could be initials."

Alice added, "Maybe the other letters are initials, too. Two sets of initials."

Finn pulled Kyle's notebook, which he'd ostensibly been studying before he got sidetracked by the baseball factoids, to his side of the table, flipped to the back, and started scribbling.

"Quit a.m.?" he suggested. "Quit in the morning? But quit what?"

We all turned to look at Emily, who knew Bryan better than

the rest of us, but she shrugged. "He was a smoker," she offered.

Finn pulled a face. "Maybe. But who plans to quit smoking on a random Wednesday morning at the end of April? And why in the morning?"

"What about the phone number?" I asked, grabbing my purse off the floor and pulling out my phone.

Finn read the numbers out loud, and I tapped them in and hit send.

The phone rang three times, then a little click indicated I'd been rolled over to voice mail. "Hello," the message began, "you've reached the Law Offices of Jackson and Ver Steeg. Our regular business hours are—" I clicked my phone closed.

"Well, I think the first three letters are initials. An attorney named Ver Steeg?"

Finn smacked his forehead with his open palm. "Of course. Kristen Ver Steeg. She and her partner, Madeline Jackson, have an office over on FM 410, across from Lantana Plaza."

Farm Road 410 snaked around the outer perimeter of Dalliance proper and featured all the new big box stores and chain restaurants that marked Dalliance's transition from "small town" to Dallas bedroom community. I'd lived in Dalliance my whole life, save for the summers I spent on Grandma Peachy's ranch just north of town, so my usual orbit didn't take me out to FM 410 all that often.

"They have a general civil litigation practice," Finn continued. "Contracts, torts, wills and estates, even a little family law."

We all looked at Emily expectantly. "The name's familiar," she conceded. "I think I've seen it on some of the documents I've received about the administrative hearing."

Alice frowned. "So if all of the pieces of the note go together, Bryan must have been quitting something that had to do with his lawyer. Maybe he was going to tell the truth, withdraw his allegations?"

Emily blew out an impatient breath. "I don't know. Honestly, the university didn't tell me more than they had to, and after he lodged a formal grievance, I was advised to keep my distance from Bryan. But I can't imagine he was backing down."

Finn nodded. "Emily's right. Bryan faced expulsion from the graduate program, and challenging Emily's decision to fail him on his exams was his only hope of holding on. He'd invested three plus years of his life into getting a Ph.D., I can't believe he'd suddenly decide to give up the fight. Besides, what's the 'AM' for? If he were going to give up his claim, why on Wednesday and why in the morning? It's just weird."

Alice squinted and got that far away look I'd come to recognize as her "peak concentration" face.

"Maybe," she said slowly, "maybe the AM is Texas A&M? Maybe he was transferring to a different grad program, so he was going to give up his effort to stay at Dickerson."

Emily looked skeptical. "I suppose it's possible, but A&M has a competitive graduate program. It's hard to imagine he could get in there after flunking his comprehensive exams here. Twice."

Alice looked crestfallen.

"It was a good guess," Bree said helpfully, earning her an acid glare from her daughter. As they say, no good deed goes unpunished.

Emily bobbed her head from side to side, seeming to weigh some idea in her mind. "Maybe he was giving up on the doctoral degree altogether and had figured out a way to pry an A.M. out of the school."

"A.M.?" Bree and I asked simultaneously.

"Artium Magister, Latin for Master of Arts. Dickerson uses the Latin terms for all their degrees, just like Harvard."

"Really?" Finn scoffed. "I mean, Dickerson is a fine school

and all, but Harvard?"

Emily shrugged. "It's all about image," she said.

"So how hard would it be for Bryan to get this other degree?" Bree asked.

Emily waggled her hand back and forth in a noncommittal gesture. "A lot of doctoral students apply for their master's degrees after they pass their comprehensive exams, and they are given the degree as a sort of formality."

"But Bryan didn't pass the exam," Alice said.

"Exactly. But if a student isn't going on for the full Ph.D., the graduate school will let him write a thesis, a sort of abbreviated version of the dissertation, instead of taking the exam. Bryan's been working on a project since he got here, one he planned to turn into his dissertation eventually. Technically, he would need my signature as one of his advisers to get the A.M. degree." She frowned, and turned to Finn. "Remember the whole brouhaha with Dr. Howell?"

He shook his head.

"Oh, of course not. That would have been before you moved back to town. Dr. Howell was a very unpopular dean of the business school. The entire faculty hated him, but the Board of Trustees was afraid to fire him because they were worried he'd sue."

"For what?" I asked.

"Who knows? Discrimination of some sort, breach of contract, whatever. Just something to drag the university into court. Anyway, the school made him disappear by creating this new job for him: Vice President for Global Outreach, or something like that."

"So they promoted him to get rid of him?" Finn asked incredulously.

"I guess technically it was a promotion. But he doesn't do anything. They fixed up a nice office for him in the chapel building, they pay his salary, and he doesn't do squat. Ever."

"Seriously?" Kyle asked. He'd grown so quiet since his discovery that I'd almost forgotten he was there. But the prospect of getting paid to do nothing was enough to drag him into the conversation.

Emily nodded earnestly. "Seriously. The speculation is that the Board of Trustees thought it would be temporary, that Howell would use his time to find a real job at another school. Pride and all that. But they overestimated his desire to work. Apparently, Howell's perfectly happy to putter around his office, go to lunch at the faculty club, and pull out his regalia for graduation. The rumor is that he spends his days trolling old census records, working on his family's genealogy."

Bree waved her hands above her head. "Hello? This little episode of Dickerson Insider is all very interesting, but what does it have to do with Bryan Campbell."

"I was just thinking," Emily said, "that if the school was anxious enough to get rid of Bryan, they might have been willing to fudge the requirements a bit. Give him his masters without my approval."

Alice sighed expressively. "I bet the administration would do just about anything to get rid of him. 'Here, take the degree, just don't let the door hit you on the ass on your way out.'"

Emily chuckled darkly. "Exactly. It wouldn't be the first time the dons of Dickerson ignored their principles in order to get rid of a troublemaker."

Someone, though, had gone beyond fudging rules to get rid of Bryan. Someone had killed him.

Ten

My cousin Bree adores karaoke.

Me, I can't carry a tune in a bucket, so I sit back, babysit her cocktails, and bask in her reflected glory.

That particular Wednesday, she donned a bright orange tube top and tight skirt, threw on a hot pink shrug for modesty, teased her fire-engine hair up to Jesus, and greeted her admiring fans at the Bar None with a pageant-worthy wave and a shower of blown kisses. Her platform sandals added three inches to her already statuesque height, and her hair spray added another four. A strange stillness descended on the crowd as she moved through, a sort of hushed reverence as every male eye tracked her progress.

I hung back with Finn and Emily. There was a subtle intensity to Emily's features. I'd seen the same expression on Alice's face many times, including the first time she watched my new French pot ice cream freezer work its magic on simple vanilla bean flavored custard. Emily and Alice shared some fundamental inquisitiveness, some innate drive that made them alert to new puzzles and challenges.

And apparently karaoke night at the Bar None was a puzzle. Or a challenge.

Bree cozied up to the bar, spreading her arms and leaning on it as though she owned the joint, while Finn pulled out bar stools for me and Emily.

Andi Talmidge worked the bar, but she looked more like she ought to be shelving paperbacks at the local library. A fireplug of a woman with neatly permed gray hair and a tidy mauve tracksuit, she bustled about in her bright white running shoes, the look of fierce determination on her face rarely wavering.

"Bree!" she cried, one of her rare smiles lighting up her face. "Scarlett O'Hara?"

"You know it," Bree said, leaning across the bar to give Andi a brief hug. "And throw in a couple extra cherries, if you don't mind." Bree usually stuck to margaritas and beer, but when she sang she always opted for the syrupy sweet of Southern Comfort and cranberry juice. She claimed it helped her stay on pitch. Sort of the redneck version of warm water with honey and lemon.

"And for you folks?"

"Beer," Finn said. "Something in a bottle. Surprise me."

"Beer," I said. "Light, in the bottle. Maybe a Pearl?"

Emily cocked her head and studied the real estate behind the bar. She wrinkled her nose a bit.

I'd never paid much attention to how the Bar None smelled, other than to note the obvious pall of grease from the deep fat fryer, but that little twitch of distaste made me sniff more closely. Beneath the comforting smells of onion rings and barbecue sauce lay the sour scent of hops and softening citrus fruit, underscored by the tang of mildew from old bar mops. The bar smelled like the bottom of a hamper.

Suddenly, beer didn't sound so appetizing.

"Mineral water, please," Emily said. "Light ice, and a squeeze of lemon."

Andi bent forward, a rusty bark of laughter escaping her lips. "Sure thing, Princess." She trundled off, shaking her head as she went.

Emily glared at Finn. "What's wrong with water?"

Bree patted her on the back. "Nothing wrong with water. But the only bottles behind that bar are filled with booze. You'll have to live with water from the soda gun."

Emily masked her distress at this news quickly, but not before we all saw it. Bree, Finn, and I all cracked up.

"Sorry, Em," Finn said. "Welcome to Dalliance."

Emily straightened her spine. "It's not like I was born with a silver spoon in my mouth. I don't mind a little tap water. I can even do without the lemon." She softened her comment with a self-deprecating smile.

"That's my girl," Finn said, looping his arm around her neck and giving her a squeeze.

Andi delivered our drinks, and we raised our glasses and bottles in a toast before Bree set out to put her name on the performance list. She tended to favor '80s songs—Madonna, Cyndi Lauper, Pat Benatar—but that night she'd decided to go disco with Gloria Gaynor's anthem, "I Will Survive."

Finn and Emily started a slow waltz down memory lane, laughing over a polka band at some lounge in Minnesota. Feeling like a third wheel, I let my eyes roam the bar searching for familiar faces. Danny Tibert from the Dalliance PD was on the stage, rocking back and forth awkwardly as he warbled out a Phil Collins tune. I saw Vonda Hudson from the 911 call center sharing a pitcher with Karla Faye Hoffstead, who'd been doing my hair since my junior prom. And there was Ted and Shelley Alrecht, at their usual table near the stage. By the look on Shelley's face, they were in the "fight" stage of their complicated nightly ritual of emotional tug-of-war.

Just beyond Ted and Shelley, at a table in the shadows at the corner of the stage, I saw a familiar face. I probably wouldn't have noticed him, but he looked out of place among the cowboy hats and T-shirts. His narrow head and high, cheek boned face were clean shaven, and he was dressed more for cat burglary than karaoke. He wore a black turtleneck, and a chunky gold watch glinted on his wrist as he raised a highball glass for a drink.

A blonde woman sat at his table, her back to me. She must have said something, because he leaned in and tipped his head to hear her better amidst the din of the crowd and Danny Tibert's caterwauling. That's when I recognized him, the gesture jarring loose the memory of him at Bryan's funeral.

Whatever his companion said made him laugh, and he rested his hand over hers. Even from across the room, I could tell it was no casual touch. His fingers lingered over hers, then slipped across her wrist in a delicate caress.

The woman's attention remained fixed on the man, and I couldn't see her face at all. But given her hair color and the petite size of her frame, I knew she wasn't the woman who had accompanied him at the funeral.

I leaned over and tapped Emily on the arm. "Who's that?"

Keeping my hand below my waist, I pointed as subtly as I could. She followed my gesture, and I saw the corners of her mouth tense.

"Jonas Landry," she said. "Our fearless leader."

Ah, the chair of the English Department.

"Is that his wife?" I asked.

Emily rolled her eyes. "No. It's the chippie du jour."

"He's single?" I could have sworn the woman at the funeral was his wife. They'd seemed to be together, and who brought a date to a funeral?

"Oh, no," Emily said. "He's married. That's just not his wife. That's one of many girlfriends."

I confess, I was dumbstruck for a moment.

Don't get me wrong. My daddy had two wives, and my ex tomcatted around town for over fifteen years, so infidelity didn't shock me. But this guy was trotting out his girlfriend in front of God and everyone.

My surprise must have shown on my face, because Emily laughed, an unexpectedly girlish giggle.

"Isn't he worried about getting caught?" I asked.

"The only people he'd be worried about, well, they aren't likely to be at the Bar None for karaoke night."

I thought about what Reggie had said, about how Bryan's working relationship with Jonas Landry had gone south in the fall. Maybe Bryan knew about Jonas's harem.

I suggested as much to Emily.

"Oh, I'm sure Bryan knew," Emily said with a nod. "Everyone did. It's one of the worst kept secrets at Dickerson."

"Does his wife know?" I asked, half dreading the response. I'd played the part of unwitting wife for years before I took a turn at "woman scorned." I couldn't recommend either role.

"Sally? Sure. She's on the faculty at Dickerson. Ironically enough, she teaches women's studies."

"Doesn't she care?"

Emily shrugged. "She's not thrilled about it. I know the other female faculty talk smack about her for putting up with such a dog. But she's not about to leave him."

"Why not?" Finn asked. I'd been so caught up in the drama of Jonas and Sally Landry, I'd almost forgotten he was there.

"The Landrys have turned the two body problem on its head," Emily replied.

I signaled to Andi that I needed another beer. "You lost me."

Emily leaned into her story. "Academic couples face something we call the two body problem. See, in any given year, there are only a handful of jobs at each academic institution, and schools are often geographically isolated from each other. So if you have two would-be professors trying to land jobs together at the same time...well, it's really hard. A lot of times, one member of the couple leaves teaching in favor of some other profession. Or some crap school takes advantage of their desperation to be together and snaps up professors they shouldn't be able to get."

"I'd never thought about that," I said. "But how did the Landrys deal with the problem?"

"Easy. Jonas is incredibly successful. He publishes like crazy, and now he's got this book that's getting him national attention. Dickerson will do anything to keep him. Even continue to promote his wife."

Ah. "So Sally's riding Jonas's coattails," I said.

"Exactly. She's bright enough, but she's not a very good teacher and none of her articles have hit. She published her dissertation, but with a third-rate academic press and it was panned by the reviewers. Basically, she'd have been out on her ear years ago if the administration wasn't so desperate to hold on to Jonas."

Finn drained the last of his beer. "Sally puts up with Jonas cheating, because without him she'd lose her job."

"Bingo."

"But," Finn said, "why does Jonas stay in the relationship if he's so obviously unhappy?"

"Who says he's unhappy? Sally is a good hostess and can make intelligent small talk at university events. Plus, being married makes Jonas more attractive to the conservative members of the school's Board of Trustees. And, of course, there's no better way to keep your girlfriend from making demands on your time than by saying, 'Gee, honey, I'd love to watch a chick flick and cuddle on the couch, but I gotta get home to my wife.'"

Finn narrowed his eyes and gazed across the bar at Jonas Landry with something akin to admiration. "Brilliant," he said.

I elbowed him—gently—in the gut. "Despicable."

"Despicably brilliant. Or maybe brilliantly despicable. Either way, this guy's got it all figured out."

Emily bobbed her head from side to side. "Mmmmm, not entirely. Like I said, the Board of Trustees of Dickerson is pretty conservative. A lot of good Southern Baptists. A good old-fashioned sex scandal might tarnish the golden boy over there enough that the Board would give him the boot.

"But," she added, waving her glass in a general salute to the Bar None, "the Board of Trustees does not do honky-tonk."

For a second, we couldn't hear a thing as the crowd went wild. Bree had taken the stage and slipped the shrug from her shoulders to reveal her wondrous buxomness in her tangerine tube top. She knew just where to position herself, so the lights turned her hair to a fiery halo and cast her face in seductive shadow.

She stood very still, her head bowed, until the room grew quiet.

Into the near silence, the dramatic opening chord sounded followed by the trilling piano run. Bree raised her head, her gaze searching into the distance above the audience's heads.

"First I was afraid, I was petrified," she sang, her voice clear and vulnerable. She built the emotion of the song like a virtuoso, until the high-hat disco beat kicked in and my cousin's sexy hips began to sway back in forth in time.

The crowd went crazy, hooting and hollering as Bree belted out Gloria Gaynor's defiant lyrics. The song crescendoed to its powerful conclusion, and Bree brought the house down.

As applause rocked the room, Emily hopped down from her stool and raised her arms. "Wooo!" she screamed, bouncing up and down like a groupie at a Bon Jovi concert.

She took her seat again, leaning forward to close the distance between us. "She's amazing," Emily said, yelling to be heard above the demands for an encore.

"Oh, yeah. She's got a voice on her," I replied.

To be honest, a lot of Bree's appeal was pure showmanship. If you closed your eyes, you could hear when she went flat. But she could put on quite a show, no doubt about it.

"About Jonas," I said, dragging the conversation back to more pressing matters, "if Bryan knew that the Board of Trustees wouldn't approve of Landry's shenanigans, do you think he might have blackmailed him?"

Emily's smile faded, and I felt bad for bringing her back to earth. The whole point of the evening was to give her a break from her worries, and I kept reminding her all about them.

"I doubt it," she said. "I mean, maybe. But if Bryan was blackmailing Jonas, it was probably for advancement in the graduate program. And he got what he wanted from Jonas."

I looked at her sharply, and I saw the moment she realized what she'd said. Without meaning to, she'd intimated that Landry had voted to pass Bryan on his exam. Whatever the vote, it hadn't been unanimous. And if Landry supported Bryan passing, that meant Emily's insistence on failing the boy would look all the more suspicious.

"Let's just drop it," Emily said.

I nodded. After all, we were out to have fun.

But even Bree's sex-on-a-stick rendition of Madonna's "Material Girl" couldn't banish my feeling that I'd learned something important at the Bar None.

Eleven

The next morning, as I nursed a bit of a sore head from my evening at the Bar None, Cal McCormack called and asked me to meet him for lunch at Erma's Fry by Night Diner. I had a horrible feeling he wanted to discuss Alice's ill-fated espionage attempt. As much as I wanted to weasel out of it, the goody-two-shoes angel who'd always whispered in my ear made me go.

Erma's is just a couple of doors down from the A-la-mode. It's not a fancy place, just a standard-issue diner with Formica tables and wobbly wooden chairs, air thick with the scent and sounds of food frying on an industrial grill. Erma's didn't serve nouvelle anything, just heaping plates of hash browns, chicken-fried steak, and cream gravy. All the food tended to shades of beige, but it was delicious.

Dr. Pepper bottles filled with plastic daisies nestled against the table caddies of off-brand artificial sweeteners and big bottles of hot sauce. The Dalliance old-timers—judges, plumbers, doctors, and cobblers—crowded the long counter that fronted the kitchen, bumping elbows as they sipped black coffee, traded gossip, and made the deals that kept the town running.

Cal and I raised some grizzled eyebrows when we took a table together near the back of the diner. He held my chair for me and handed me a vinyl covered menu.

"How's Sherbet?" he asked as he took his own seat.

I grinned. "He's better. A dumb ass, but a healthy dumb

ass."

Cal's mouth widened in a lazy smile. "He's just a little fella," he said. "He'll make better choices as he gets older."

"Really? Is that how it's supposed to work?"

"For cats," he said. He gave me a teasing wink. "For people, once a dumb ass, always a dumb ass."

"Hmmmm. That doesn't bode well for me."

"Nah, Tally, you're not a dumb ass. Just too bighearted and gullible for your own good."

"Oh?"

"Yeah, Alice vouched for you. She said the whole stunt in Bryan's office was her idea, and you didn't know what she planned."

I pulled a face. "What does that say about me, that I was duped by a teenager?"

He laughed. "It says you're human. Teenagers are ornery little buggers."

I accepted his olive branch with a smile.

"Oh, yeah?" I teased. "Have a lot of experience with ornery teenagers, do you?"

"Let's see." He held up his hand to tick off points on his fingers. "First, I was one. Second, I'm a cop. Third, I'm an uncle. Bryan was a high-achiever, but he got into his share of trouble."

He looked out over my shoulder and cleared his throat. "He was a good kid."

"I'm sorry, Cal."

"It's okay," he said, waving off my concern. "I've just been thinking a lot about him lately. You know, I was still a kid when Bryan was born. Eleven, twelve, something like that. I was working on Eagle Scouts when he became a Cub Scout. I took him camping a lot, worked on getting his badges. Dang near singed off all my arm hair trying to teach the kid to make a hobo dinner."

I laughed along with him.

"I don't know if he really enjoyed much of what we did, but he sure wanted to get those badges. The only time I was completely sure Bryan was having a good time on our camping trips was when we were making s'mores."

"He liked sweets, huh?"

"Lord, yes. But plain old regular s'mores wouldn't do. Bryan had to take everything to the next level. And so peanut butter s'mores were born."

"Mmmm. I'm hooked. Tell me more."

Cal took a sip of his water. "It's just what it sounds like. He'd smear his graham crackers with peanut butter, then top it with the chocolate bar, and finally the toasted marshmallow."

"That's genius," I said.

"His mom thought so. She tried to convince the scout leader to give Bryan an extra badge for innovation. Threw a hissy fit when the scout leader informed her that adding peanut butter to a well-known snack didn't constitute innovation."

"I'm with Marla on this one."

"I figured you would be," Cal said. He sighed. "It's good to talk about him. Marla can't go there yet. It's too soon."

"I'm glad you have good memories, Cal. And I'm glad you can share them with me."

I was getting so accustomed to thinking of Bryan as an overly ambitious young man with questionable ethics. It was good to be reminded that even this unlikeable young man had a mama who loved him, a family who loved him. That once upon a time, Bryan Campbell had been a wide-eyed little boy with no greater ambition than to earn merit badges and eat gooey sweets around a campfire.

Before either of us could grow more sentimental, the waitress sashayed up. We placed our orders without even looking at our menus: chicken-fried steak, mashed potatoes, and sweet tea for both of us. I'm sure the other food at Erma's deserved a shot, but it was hard to pass up the opportunity for the tender breaded beef smothered in peppered cream gravy.

After our waitress left, Cal got down to business. "Tally, I need some help, and I'm hoping you'll oblige."

"Of course, Cal. Anything."

He held up a cautionary hand. "Better wait till you have the facts before you wade in here. See, Marla got this idea that we should establish a scholarship in Bryan's honor."

"I think that's a lovely idea."

"It is," Cal said, "but it's going to take a lot of work. I already talked to George Gunderson and Jonas Landry at Dickerson. They were two of Bryan's advisers. They suggested having an initial fund-raising event at the very end of May."

"Why so soon?"

Cal fiddled with his silverware. "Marla's idea is to have the scholarship awarded to someone like Bryan, a serious student and a serious baseball player. So Gunderson and Landry thought it would be good to coordinate the fund-raising around the end of the collegiate baseball season. Marla's husband, Steve, thinks he can get ahold of a couple of tickets to the College World Series at the end of June, and they can be the main focus of a silent auction."

Another advantage to ordering the chicken-fried steak at Erma's is that they're constantly frying it up during the noon rush, so you never have to wait long. Our waitress swung by with two mounded platters of carbs and grease, plopped a basket of fresh rolls in the center of the table, and topped off our sweet teas.

"It sounds like a great plan," I said. "Where do I come in?"

Cal stuck his fork in his mashed potatoes, like he was going to take a bite, but just mushed the gravy around a bit.

"Marla...well, Marla's not doing too great. She can't seem to stop crying, so her doctor gave her some sort of tranquilizer. That helps with the crying, but it makes it hard for her to focus. And Steve's not much better. His sisters all live in Shreveport, so it's up to me to plan this shindig. And I'm in over my head."

"You?" I teased.

He uttered a short, mirthless laugh. "Imagine that. I can shoot straight, rope a calf, and even take down a biker hopped up on crank. But I cannot plan a party." He cocked an eyebrow. "But you can."

I paused with a forkful of spuds halfway to my mouth. "Me? Why me?"

"I know it's a big favor, Tally. But I don't know who else to ask. And I have to do this for my sister. God knows I can't give her any answers about what happened to her child."

"Do the police have any leads yet?"

He narrowed his eyes. "You asking as a friend? Or as a wannabe detective?"

That hurt. I got it, but it hurt. "As a friend. I have no intention of getting involved in the investigation."

"Hmmmm." Cal hummed thoughtfully while he buttered a roll. "For someone who's not involved, you're sure spending a lot of time with our prime suspect."

I set down my fork and folded my arms on the table in front of my plate. "Okay. First off, y'all keep telling the newspaper Emily Clowper isn't a suspect. Second, the only way you'd know how much time I was spending with Emily Clowper is if you're spying on me, and I don't appreciate that. And last, I'm not really spending time with her at all. It's Finn and Alice—who both happen to like the woman, thank you very much—and they're just spending time with her in my presence."

Cal raised his glass in an appreciative salute. "Fair enough. She's not technically a suspect, but she's the closest thing we've got. And I'm not spying on you, I'm spying on her. You just happen to be in the vicinity."

He took a sip of his tea. "As for Alice and Finn liking her, well, Alice is a kid. And Finn is a man. I'll let you draw your own conclusions."

We stared at one another, caught in a stalemate, until finally Cal reached a hand across the table.

"Truce?" he said.

I took his hand and gave it a shake. "Truce. But, seriously, if you know something about Emily that I don't know, I wish you'd tell me. I'm not wild about Alice hanging around with her as it is."

Cal tucked in to his meat. "I don't know anything but what my gut is telling me. Which is that something there just isn't right. But I was kidding about spying on her. I just heard through the grapevine that she was spending time at the A-la-mode. As much as it pains me, I'm leaving the actual investigation to my men. I'm not gonna have some lawyer claim I harassed someone and end up letting Bryan's killer go free."

Poor Cal. Forced onto the sidelines for the most important case of his life.

"Have your men gotten any leads? As a friend," I said, "I want to know."

Cal shook his head. "Nothing. No one saw anything. Or if they did, they're not saying. The murder weapon was wiped clean; there was blood on it, but no prints. And all the blood seems to be Bryan's."

His jaw clenched. I couldn't imagine having to talk about someone I'd loved in such clinical terms, but I supposed that being a cop, you learned to compartmentalize early on. Either that, or you burned out fast.

"What about blood outside the main office? The killer must have had blood on him, right?"

"Sure," he said. "And they found traces of blood in the little bathroom down the hall from the office, one of those one-person unisex things. But, again, no prints. Just evidence that someone locked him- or herself in that bathroom and washed Bryan's blood away."

"Oh, Cal." I reached around the side of the table to take his hand. He wrapped his fingers around mine, gave them a brief squeeze, and then pulled back into himself.

"What about DNA or hairs or fibers?" I asked.

"Tally, you've been watching too much TV. Other than the blood, the crime scene guys didn't find any evidence that was obviously related to the crime. There was trace all over the crime scene and the bathroom, but they're public buildings. We probably have hair from every member of the English department faculty and half the students."

"So what do you do now?"

Cal shook his head. "Not much they can do. The detectives in charge are still talking to students and faculty, everyone who knew Bryan, but unless someone other than the killer knows something—or the killer decides to confess—they're at a standstill."

"What about motive? Who would have wanted to kill Bryan?"

"Other than Emily Clowper?" Cal asked with a wry smile. Then he sighed. "I don't have the heart to tell Marla this, but it turns out people didn't really like Bryan much."

An understatement to be sure, but I didn't editorialize.

"The undergraduates thought he was too tough in the classroom, his fellow graduate students thought he was pompous and too competitive. The only people who haven't said anything bad about the kid are Landry and Gunderson."

Which begged the question whether Landry and Gunderson actually liked Bryan, or whether they had a reason to hide their animosity. From what Reggie had said, Landry and Gunderson both had issues with Bryan, but they were apparently being more diplomatic with the authorities. Again, though, it didn't seem like the time to push Cal on that question. After all, I was asking as a friend, not a meddler.

Cal pushed his food around, and then let the fork fall to the plate with a clatter. "No one liked him, but no one had a real reason to kill him. Except for Emily Clowper. And that's why she may not be an official suspect, but she's certainly in our crosshairs. Sorry, their crosshairs," he amended.

"Detective McCormack?"

I looked up to find Jonas Landry standing by our table. Up close, I saw that he had sharp features and dark, penetrating eyes behind wire-rimmed spectacles that he hadn't been wearing at the funeral or at the bar. His clothes made him stand out in the denim and seersucker crowd at Erma's: a pair a gray-pleated trousers, a long-sleeved white dress shirt, and a natty black vest buttoned high on his chest.

Cal stood up to greet the newcomer, extending a hand. "Professor Landry," he said.

"Please, call me Jonas."

"Jonas. And I'm Cal. This here is Tally Jones," he said, gesturing in my direction. "We were just talking about the benefit for Bryan's scholarship fund."

Jonas Landry offered his hand, and I reluctantly took it. I didn't much care whether Sally Landry tolerated her husband's philandering or not. I thought his behavior was pretty scummy, and I didn't particularly want to socialize with the man.

"A pleasure to meet you, Ms. Jones," he said, his voice as smooth and seductive as warm dulce de leche. "You were involved with the Honor's Day program, weren't you?"

"Yes, I run the Remember the A-la-mode. We were serving ice cream at the event. My niece, Alice Anders is a student at Dickerson."

His face lit up. "Oh, yes, Alice! I've heard excellent things about her. I'm hoping to convince her to take my seminar on mid-century European cinema next year."

"Cinema? Aren't you in the English Department?"

He chuckled, that "oh, how quaint" chuckle I was coming to loath from these academics.

"Yes, I'm actually the chair of the English Department. But my specialty is in the study of cinema. I'm a bit of a relic, I suppose"—he said, again with the chuckle of superiority— "as I am a firm believer in the auteur theory of film criticism. I study the works of great directors, authors and artists who use a visual medium to tell their story rather than the written word."

"Oh."

Cal nodded. "Jonas here wrote a book that got him on all sorts of talk shows, on NPR and such. And now it's up for a big national award."

Landry blinked rapidly three or four times. "How... how did you hear about that?"

Cal smiled. "No need to be bashful. Bryan mentioned it one evening at dinner."

The last word I would have used to describe Jonas Landry was "bashful." But he did seem taken aback by the fact that Cal knew about his work. Or the fact that Cal knew about the award. Maybe he was superstitious and didn't want to jinx his chances by talking about it.

Indeed, Jonas waved off the topic. "It's really nothing," he said. "Tell me about the plans for the benefit."

"There's not much to tell right now," Cal said. "I was just asking Tally here if she'd help with the planning."

Both men looked at me expectantly, and I did the only thing I could do.

I said yes.

Twelve

As her wedding date approached, Crystal Tompkins grew increasingly more self-possessed. I'd seen plenty of brides melt down into bratty children over their impending nuptials, but Crystal seemed more serene every day, as though she was becoming more and more confident of her feminine power.

She sat across from me at one of the A-la-mode café tables, leisurely licking a double-chocolate waffle cone while I scribbled "Crystal's Wedding" across the top of a blank legal pad.

"So tell me about this groom's shake idea," I said.

Crystal's cupid's bow mouth turned up in an enigmatic Mona Lisa smile. "All my mom," she said. "Personally, I don't care much about the tradition. It's supposed to be a gift from the bride to the groom, right? Well, trust me, I'm giving Jason a gift. Just not in public."

She licked her ice cream again, the tip of her pink tongue darting out to catch a drip of chocolate before it ran down the side of the cone. Apparently the nut didn't fall far from the tree, and Crystal had more than a trace of her mama's devilish nature.

"Well, whether it's your idea or hers, your mama's got her heart set on these milkshakes, and I want to make them special for you."

Crystal chuckled. "Oh, and I appreciate it, Ms. Jones. Jason loves ice cream, and he'll get a kick out of having his very own milkshake flavor."

"What's he like?"

"Jason?" She screwed up her features in concentration. "He's a pretty simple guy, really. Laughs a lot. He likes watching football and playing computer games, tinkering with cars. All the boy stuff."

"What about food? Anything special he likes?"

She smiled. "He's a Texas boy. Barbecue and chili and Tex-Mex. In fact, our first date was a barbecue."

"Really? Tell me about it."

"Well, I guess it wasn't our first date. I mean, we'd known each other for years, but the first time I thought 'Wow, he's cute,' was at a big barbecue we had for debate my freshman year of high school. We were going to the state championship that year, and we had this big fund-raiser."

That would have been the year that Bryan Campbell was the captain of the team. Deena had mentioned the team's triumph at Bryan's funeral.

"Anyway, we all brought food to sell. Jason brought brisket smothered in his homemade sauce."

"He made his own sauce?" That seemed pretty ambitious for a high school boy.

Crystal laughed. "He'd done 4-H and FFA for years, but Jason's not really a manly man, you know? He always gravitated to the cooking and canning competitions. His barbecue sauce is impressive."

"What's he use?"

Crystal waggled a finger at me. "Oh, now, Miz Jones, you know that a Texas man won't share his barbecue recipe with anyone but his horse."

"Mmmm-hmmm. But something tells me Jason wouldn't dare keep secrets from you."

She winked. "I'll give you a hint. His secret ingredient is Dr.

Pepper."

"Really?"

"Yep," she said with a satisfied nod. "Dublin Dr. Pepper."

Dr. Pepper is the unofficial state beverage of Texas. Older than Pepsi, RC, or even Coca-Cola, Dr. Pepper originated in Waco, Texas. The Dublin variety of Dr. Pepper is made with the old formula, using cane sugar instead of corn syrup. It's harder to find, but worth the hunt. I jotted "Dr. Pepper" on my legal pad.

"What did you bring to that barbecue?" I asked.

"I brought a red raspberry pie. My mom had just taught me to make pastry crust, and we had raspberries out the yin yang that year. Jason always told me that my pie caught his eye, but my smile won his heart."

I sighed as I scribbled "raspberry" on my notepad. Such a sweet story.

"You've been dating a long time."

She shrugged. "Yeah. A lot of our friends figured we'd get married right out of high school. But we both wanted to wait."

"That was smart. It's hard to know whether high school crushes are real love or not."

Crystal looked at me like I was nuts. "Oh, we knew it was real love. Love is love, no matter how old you are. But we both have plans, ambitions. We were afraid that if we got married, we'd start feeling obligated to buy a house and have babies and all the rest of it. And then we might not both get to go to law school."

Jason had just finished his third year and would be taking the bar exam later in the summer, and Crystal planned to start school in the fall.

"Weren't you afraid that Jason would meet some girl up at Tech?"

That mysterious womanly smile returned. "No, ma'am. I

always knew Jason would come back to me. If it's meant to be, it's meant to be."

I envied her that certainty. Maybe if I'd been as confident about Finn's love, certain he would come back to Dalliance for me, I wouldn't have married Wayne Jones. But then again, maybe what Finn and I had wasn't as strong or as real as the love Crystal and Jason shared.

I'd learned the hard way that there was no point living in the past, second-guessing the choices I'd made.

"I never doubted Jason," Crystal continued, the smile fading from her lips, "but this whole thing with Bryan has made me glad we're getting married now. Not waiting even longer. Jason, I trust. Life, not so much."

"Your mom said you and Jason knew Bryan pretty well."

"As well as anyone could know Bryan."

"What do you mean?"

"I mean he was a tough nut. He had big dreams, wanted to be important and make money. But most people want to be good at something particular, like Jason wants to be a really great prosecutor, and my mom wants to be an amazing caterer, and my stepdad wants to raise the very best horses. Bryan didn't seem to care what he was successful at, as long as he was successful."

"There's nothing wrong with that," I said.

She tilted her head, a skeptical expression on her face. "I guess not," she conceded, "but it meant Bryan was easily distracted. He'd be your friend, but then if he saw a better path to getting ahead, he'd never talk to you again. He wasn't mean, just driven."

"That sounds like a lonely life."

She nodded. "Last time I saw Bryan was at a holiday party. A bunch of debaters got together and hit the Bar None for cocktails a couple of weeks before Christmas, right after a lot of us came back from school on the semester break. We were doing the whole 'What are you up to?' thing, and we got to Bryan. Everyone else had talked about school and significant others, even a few babies and weddings, and Bryan starts telling us about his five-year plan. How he's going to graduate and get a postdoc and write a novel and sell a screenplay."

I frowned, not sure what point she was trying to make.

"The rest of us were talking about what we were doing, then, at that time. Bryan never even mentioned what he was working on at Dickerson, his dissertation, his classes, anything. It was all what he planned to do. That was Bryan in a nutshell, so busy scheming three steps ahead of the game that he never got to enjoy what he'd already accomplished."

"Maybe he didn't want to talk about school because of all the trouble he was having with Dr. Clowper."

Crystal scrunched her face. "Nah. Jason asked him about that, pulled him aside and said, 'Hey, I know some lawyers if you need one.' Bryan waved him off, said there was nothing to worry about, he had bigger fish to fry."

"Just because he didn't want to talk about his troubles with his old friends, doesn't mean they weren't weighing on him," I insisted.

Crystal balled up a napkin and scrubbed at an imaginary spot on the cafe table. "I guess you're right. And he did get pretty drunk that night. Hooked up with a girl who called him 'Dr. Campbell.'" She snorted. "He left with her, without even saying good-bye to the rest of us."

"Was she his girlfriend?" If Bryan had a girlfriend, the police needed to know. Maybe she wouldn't be a suspect, but she might have information about other people who had bones to pick with Bryan.

"No," Crystal said, her voice ringing with certainty. "Definitely not a girlfriend. Just a hookup."

It crossed my mind to ask her how she knew, but I wasn't sure I'd understand. Alice's generation had strange ideas about boy-girl relationships, about what constituted dating as opposed to just "hooking up."

Crystal glanced down at her wrist. "Oh, dear, I have to run. Jason was supposed to drop off the deposit check for the band, but he got a part-time job with a firm in town, so now it's up to me."

"That's good news about the job," I said.

"Yeah. He's taking the bar in July, so he needs to study, but he's hoping that Madeline and Kristen will hire him on permanently in the fall."

"Jackson and Ver Steeg?"

"You've heard of the firm?"

I smiled. Dalliance really was a small town. "Only good things," I said.

"Do you have enough for the milkshakes?"

I looked at my notepad. Dr. Pepper and raspberries. Huh. "Do you trust me?"

Crystal grinned. "If that cone was a fair representation of your work, then, yeah, I trust you."

"Well, if you trust me and you're willing to be a bit adventurous, I think I have you covered."

Thirteen

Emily and Finn had already staked out a spot at the back of the A-la-mode that Friday evening, and both were busy tapping away at their laptop keyboards, when Alice stormed in. She covered the distance to their table in long, purposeful strides and let her backpack drop to the floor with a menacing thud.

"Hey, kiddo," Finn said as he raised his head. "How's tricks…?" He let the question trail off as he took in Alice's furious expression.

"Alice?" Emily said. "What's going on?"

"Why don't you tell me?" Alice ground out.

By that point, Bree and Kyle had joined me at the counter, and we watched the drama unfolding before us with cautious concern.

"What do you mean?" Finn asked.

"I mean that Dr. Clowper has been lying to us all."

"Alice," Finn said, his tone stern, almost fatherly, "that's a serious allegation."

"I know," Alice said, "but it's the truth. Dr. Clowper is a liar."

A fine tremor of rage vibrated through Alice's whole body. Bree took a few tentative steps toward her child, but I reached out to stop her. As angry as she was, Alice was apt to lash out at Bree if she interfered, and then we'd never get to the bottom of this.

Emily met Alice's fury with stone-faced calm. "I have not lied to you, Alice."

"Really?" Alice raised her chin in challenge. "I know about you and Reggie."

The color leached from Emily's face, leaving her ashen. Ghostly.

"What are you talking about?" Finn said.

Alice and Emily simply stared at each other.

"Seriously," Finn said, clearly exasperated, "one of you needs to start talking. Now."

Emily cut her eyes in his direction, a furtive glance. The tip of her tongue peeked out and moistened her lips. I thought she might explain, but then she clammed up again.

Finally, Alice propped her hands on her hips and turned her attention to Finn.

"After class today, Reggie and I met to go over the grading rubric for the midterm. The message light on his phone was blinking, so he put it on speaker so he could take notes while he listened to the messages. One of the messages was from Dr. Clowper." Her voice hitched, and she cleared her throat before continuing. "She said, 'Hey, babe.'"

It took a second before the penny dropped. A teacher didn't call her student "babe." Not unless they were engaged in some serious extracurricular activities.

Finn's eyes widened in surprise, and he looked at Emily for confirmation. She couldn't hold his gaze for long. And while she didn't say a word, the misery on her face was eloquent.

I couldn't hold Bree back anymore. She dashed around the counter and to her baby's side. But when she tried to wrap her arms around Alice's shoulders, Alice shook her off and stepped toward Emily.

"You knew," she said.

"Knew what?" Emily asked.

Alice's eyes narrowed. "You knew I liked him. And you never said a word. Just let me make a fool of myself by asking him out and getting turned down flat." Most of the time, Alice was the smartest person in the room, so it was easy to forget she was a teenager, just turned seventeen in May, and her world revolved around Alice.

"I didn't—" Emily protested, but Alice rushed on.

"Did you two have a good laugh over that? Poor, silly Alice mooning over a guy who's way out of her league."

"Of course not," Emily said. She reached for Alice's hand, but Alice jerked away. "It wasn't my place to interfere."

"If not yours, then whose place was it?" Emily physically flinched at the venom in Alice's voice. "I know you're my teacher and not my friend, but what kind of person does that? Sits back and lets someone get hurt? Watches a crime being committed and says nothing? Watches an accident and doesn't get help?"

Emily's expression had shifted from contrition to puzzlement. Something Alice had said had caught her attention, gotten the wheels in her brain turning.

She leaned forward. "What if—" she began, but Alice stepped back and turned her head away dramatically.

"Whatever," she hissed.

She spun on her heel and stalked back to the front door. "I'll be back to help clean up later, Aunt Tally," she threw over her shoulder before yanking open the door and exiting as furiously as she'd entered.

Kyle was hot on her heels, hesitating only briefly at the door until I gave him a little nod of approval, and then he shoved out the door behind her.

In Alice's wake, a consuming silence filled the A-la-mode, the sort of airless hush that fills the eye of a storm.

Hurricane Finn hit with a wallop. "Bryan was telling the truth."

Emily, who continued to watch the door through which Alice had disappeared as if it were a puzzle to be solved, snapped her head around toward him. "Bryan was not telling the truth," she insisted.

"You slept with a student."

"Yes," she said softly. And then again, with more force. "Yes. I did. But not with Bryan Campbell."

"Really?"

She glanced away for a moment before looking Finn square in the eye. "Really. I never slept with him, never propositioned him, never even made an improper comment in his presence."

"So it's just a coincidence that he accuses you of sexually harassing him, when you happen to be sexually harassing another student."

Emily sat down hard, as though Finn's words were a physical blow. "I didn't sexually harass Reggie. Our," she hesitated, "our relationship was consensual. It didn't start until after he took his exams, and until he finishes his dissertation, I don't officially have any authority over him."

Officially. She was splitting hairs, and we all knew it. If her affair with this Reggie kid was entirely kosher, she wouldn't have taken such pains to keep it hidden.

"And it's not a coincidence," she continued. "Bryan knew about Reggie and me. He called Reggie one night, late, about a paper they were coauthoring. We were asleep, and Reggie's phone was on the bedside table. I was barely awake, and I answered it without thinking." She sucked in a pained breath. "As soon as Bryan found out, I realized how stupid I was being and I ended things with Reggie. I've barely spoken to him since then, and I've kept our relationship purely professional."

'Hey babe,' didn't sound professional to me, but I knew how hard it was to change the way we thought about people. Wayne Jones and I had been divorced for over a year, and I still sometimes thought of him as my husband. Habits of the heart are the toughest to break.

Finn laughed. "I know you're not a country girl, but surely you've heard the old saying about closing the barn door after the horses have gotten out."

"Finn," Emily pleaded, but he held up a hand to forestall any explanation.

"If you were having sex," he sneered, "with Reggie but not with Bryan, why didn't Bryan report you for the sin you were committing instead of making one up?"

"Because at most my relationship with Reggie would get me fired. That wouldn't help Bryan. He'd still be thrown out of the doctoral program for failing his comps. But if I pressured him for sexual favors, he might be able to hang on. And the reality of my relationship with Reggie would make his allegations more credible. As you yourself have so deftly illustrated." She waved her hand as though she wanted to dismiss that particular subject. "I think—"

"Enough," Finn snapped. He closed up his laptop and shoved it into its carrying case. "I've got to call it a day. I've got a lot to digest, and we have a staff meeting at the *News-Letter* first thing in the morning."

Emily sat up, startled. Finn smiled grimly. "Don't worry, Em. I won't mention your indiscretion to my colleagues. If anyone's going to get this scoop, it's going to be me. And I develop a story, get all the facts, before I print. So you can rest easy."

He slung his laptop bag over his shoulder, plowed his fingers through the swoop of dark hair that perpetually fell in his eyes, and strode out.

Beside me, Bree slipped her apron off. "I'm gonna go find the kids before Kyle comforts Alice right out of her panties," she said softly.

That left me alone with Emily Clowper. I had this weird sense of déjà vu, like I was watching my own life unfold again, this time from a distance. Almost exactly nineteen years earlier, I'd disappointed Finn Harper and watched him storm out of my life. Emily and I might not have much in common, but at that moment, I was uncomfortably aware of how she must feel.

"He'll get over it," I said, though I was all too aware of Finn's ability to hold a grudge.

Emily laughed humorlessly. "No he won't." She looked at me, not as a professor or as a rival, but as a fellow woman. "One of the things I loved about him was that overblown sense of integrity of his."

"Finn?" I was genuinely startled.

"Yes, Finn. It's the Harper Way or the highway," she said, and I got the sense she'd said it before. Probably to Finn. When they were both naked.

Ack.

To clear my mind of that image, I pulled a diet soda out of the cooler. "Can I get you something?" I asked.

"No, thanks," Emily said. "I'm—"

"Diabetic," I finished. "I remember."

Emily laughed. "Am I that predictable?"

I returned her smile. "Pretty much. But we have soda and juice and water. I think Bree even has a block of pepper-jack cheese and a box of crackers in the back, if you're hungry."

"Actually, I was going to say that I'm stuffed. Finn and I went to the new Thai place for dinner." Just mentioning his name chased her smile away.

I popped the top on my can and sat down across from her. "You know, when he was in high school, Finn was a total rebel. He drank and listened to punk music and even got a tattoo."

She nodded. "The little anarchy symbol on his shoulder blade. Yeah, he told me about that."

I wondered if he'd told her that I'd been with him that night, driving his Scirocco since he had to do shots of whiskey to work up the courage to face the needle.

"He's not all that interested in other people's rules," she continued, "but he has his own sense of right and wrong. And when it comes to his own personal code of conduct, he's as rigid as they come. Like I said, that's one of the things that drew me to him. His strong principles."

I took a sip of my soda. "He said the same thing about you," I admitted. I didn't particularly want to play intermediary in their relationship, even if it was purely platonic, but I felt so bad for her. "He said that you were a straight shooter."

Hand to God, I meant to make her feel better, but my words had the opposite effect. She buried her face in her hands. "I really blew it," she said.

"Why?" I asked.

"Why, what?"

"Why have a fling with a student? I mean, I'm not judging here, but it doesn't seem like a very smart life choice. And you're obviously a really smart lady."

That elicited a bark of wry laughter. She lowered her hands and sat up straighter. "Even 'smart ladies' do stupid things sometimes. I think there's a self-help book with that very title." She shrugged. "What can I say? I was lonely and stressed out."

I must have looked skeptical, because she rolled her eyes. "I know most people think college professors have a pretty cushy life. I guess in a lot of respects we do. But it's hard, frustrating work, and it's never ever done. First, there's the teaching. We're supposed to be rigorous, demanding, but then, at the end of the semester, the administration lets students evaluate us. Do you think students like rigorous, demanding teachers? Most don't. Most want an easy "A." So they slam you on your evaluations, and the same administrator who told you to be tough tells you

you're a bad teacher because the students don't love you."

I had to admit, that didn't seem fair.

"Even if I please my students, it's not enough. If I want to keep my job, I have to publish scholarly articles. Publish or perish, as they say. But I can't control whether my work gets published or not. I can spend months working on an article, submit it to a journal, and two anonymous reviewers give me completely contradictory reasons for why it sucks. You know who those reviewers are? Other scholars, who are competing to get their articles in the exact same journals. I don't get a chance to explain why they're wrong and I'm right, I just have to lump it."

She looked around at the A-la-mode. "Running a small business must be frustrating, too. You can make great ice cream—and Finn raves about your ice cream, by the way—but you can't make people buy it. It's the same for me. I can give kids a good education, but I can't make them like it. And I can write insightful scholarship, but I can't make anyone publish it."

I confess, I'm a sucker for compliments. That little bone she threw me, about Finn liking my ice cream, went a long way in softening my heart toward her. And it sounded like we had more in common than I ever would have imagined.

"Anyway," she said, "the academic world is stressful and isolating."

"Did you ever think about getting a pet?" I asked. Sherbet had become quite a feature in my life, and it seemed to me that a dog or cat beat an inappropriate sexual liaison by a long shot.

She laughed for real at that. "Actually I did. I had a dog when I was a girl, a Great Pyrenees named Bella. She was huge and shaggy and went tearing off after squirrels every chance she got." She smiled, a bittersweet twist of the lips that somehow softened her whole face. "I always wanted to get another dog, another Great Pyrenees, just like Bella."

"So why didn't you?"

"I was waiting to get tenure," she said. "Right now, I work too many hours to take care of a pet. And if I don't get tenure, and I have to move, it will be so much harder with a dog, especially a big one."

I guess that made sense, but it sounded mighty sad to me.

"It's the same reason I don't date, really. I spend all my time on campus, so it's tough to meet people who aren't a part of that world. Even when I do, they have no idea what I do all day, and they're usually not very interested in hearing about it. I mean, everyone likes ice cream, but most people don't want to discuss feminist poetry over beers, you know? Reggie actually thinks my work is fascinating. He thinks I'm fascinating."

And that sealed the deal. Emily Clowper might hale from a big city, and possess a fancy education. She might have a trendy haircut, wear funky glasses, and have the body of a twenty-year-old. But beneath all that gloss and sophistication, she had the same fundamental need to be appreciated that we all have. I couldn't deny that basic female bond.

I reached across the table to cover her hand with my own. She startled, but she didn't pull away. "Emily," I said, "it will be okay."

At first she studied my face from behind her hipster glasses, the naturalist observing an unusual insect. The anthropologist and the headhunter. And I retracted my hand.

But then she smiled again, not laughing at me or even commiserating with me. Thanking me.

"It will be okay," she said with a small nod. "In fact, I think I know how to make everything okay now."

But something in her eyes told me she didn't believe it any more than I did.

Fourteen

Emily had left by the time Bree returned to the shop with Alice. I'd sent her off with a promise to stop waiting and get a dog, and a promise to give Finn a couple of days to cool off and then call him again.

"I sent Kyle packing," Bree said. "If that boy wants to graduate in June, he's got to spend less time moping around this joint and more time cracking his school books."

Kyle Mason had a long rap sheet as a general juvenile delinquent. He'd started working at the Remember the A-la-mode the summer before, just after I purchased Dave's Dippery and relaunched it as an upscale ice cream parlor, so that he could pay court-ordered restitution for a mailbox smashing spree. Even with the piddly wages I could afford to pay him, he'd managed to make good on his debt, and I felt confident he'd only continued scooping ice cream because of his excruciating unrequited crush on Alice. He'd never get past first base with my brainiac niece if he didn't make nice with his teachers and graduate.

"This one," Bree continued, jerking a thumb at Alice, "insisted on coming back to help."

"You really can take off, Alice," I said. "Aren't finals next week?" She nodded glumly. "Or at least go home and get some sleep."

"No, I want to make caramel," she said, her lower lip

drifting suspiciously close to a pout.

While I found a certain Zen pleasure in the homely act of making ice cream, and Bree just liked to sneak licks and nibbles, the process appealed to Alice on a more intellectual level. The alchemy of cold and motion transforming humble ingredients— sugar, milk, fruit—into something as decadent as our Peach Melba ice cream intrigued her.

But as much as Alice enjoyed the chemistry of ice cream, caramel was her favorite: the individual crystals of sugar breaking down into a whole new substance, through an inversion process scientists didn't entirely understand, followed by the spectacle of the cold cream hitting the hot sugar syrup and frothing to fill the pan, and finally the Maillard reaction turning protein and sugar into golden deliciousness. She said it made her feel like one of Shakespeare's witches.

"'Double, double toil and trouble,'" I said.

A faint smile lit her face and she rubbed her hands together. "'Fire burn, and cauldron bubble,'" she finished.

We didn't technically need more salted caramel sauce, but it wouldn't hurt to lay in some extra. "Go ahead," I said.

The three of us worked in silence, Alice tending the caramel, Bree washing up, and me packing pints to stock the retail freezer, until Alice let forth a mighty yawn, the sort of yawn that used to herald imminent collapse when she was a toddler. It was well past midnight, a good two hours after her emotional confrontation with Emily, and the poor child had to be dead on her feet.

Bree pried the spoon from her daughter's fingers, physically pointed her toward the back door, and gave her a little shove. "Go."

"Yes, ma'am," Alice mumbled, and headed out, stripping her apron as she went.

As soon as the door clicked closed, Bree sighed. "What am I

going to do with her, Tally?"

"Love her."

"More than my own breath," she said. "But just when I figure she's grown, she doesn't need her mama anymore, a boy hurts her heart or a friend betrays her, and she's my baby again. Yet the second I get back in the swing of mothering her, she's pushing me away."

I laughed. "Bree Michaels, you just described dang near every mother-daughter relationship in the history of forever. I don't think it'll ever stop. Right up to the day my mama died, she and Grandma Peachy were doing that dance. And you and Aunt Jenny spend five minutes together and either she's smothering you or you're pitching a fit. Why should you and Alice be any different?"

"I guess you're right." Bree sighed again. "I'm just so dang worried about her."

"Of course you are. I am, too. But we have to trust that she's a smart girl, smarter than the two of us put together, and probably more sensible to boot."

Bree chuckled as she gave the caramel sauce one last stir, then whacked the spoon on the edge of the pot a couple of times. She opened her mouth to say something, but tinny music cut her off, some foreboding operatic thing that would have made me think of marauding hordes of barbarians if it weren't coming from the hamper where we dumped our aprons at the end of the day.

Alice had apparently left her phone in her pocket again. She'd already lost one that way, when it got thrown in the washer with blazing hot water and a scoop of Borax.

Bree sighed and dug the phone out of the laundry. She frowned at the screen and declined the call. She'd just started to tuck the phone into her own pants pocket, when the barbarians returned.

With a huff, Bree flipped open the phone. "Hello? No, Dr. Clowper, this is her mama." She caught my eye and made a gagging motion with her finger. "Alice is on her way home. It's been a really long day, and I don't think she wants to talk to you just now. Yes, she needs to sleep, too. Maybe I can have her call you tomorrow. No matter how important it is, it will wait until morning."

I couldn't hear Emily's side of the conversation, but whatever she was saying did not impress Bree. Her lips thinned and her nostrils pinched in like they did when she was annoyed.

"Tim who?" she snapped. "Is he another one of your boy toys?" There was a beat of silence. "Do you have Tim's keys, or does he have yours? Because I don't think you should be driving. And why are you whispering?" Bree extended the pinky and thumb of her left hand and raised it to her lips in the universal sign for "drunk as a skunk."

A sense of unease began plucking at the corner of my consciousness. I couldn't put it into words right then, but something seemed off.

"Money? Whose money? Listen, I can barely hear you. Why don't you go lay down now, get some sleep. We can straighten out the whole key situation in the morning." There was a beat of silence, during which Emily must have been talking. "Who did what?" Another pause, and then Bree smacked the heel of her hand against her forehead. "No, I don't have any candy," she ground out.

My uneasiness erupted into full-fledged alarm. I snatched an old work schedule off the door of the walk-in, rooted around in my apron pocket for a pen, and scrawled the word "DIABETIC" in big loopy letters. I held it in front of Bree's face and watched as her expression morphed from annoyance to confusion to wide-eyed panic.

"Dr. Clowper," she snapped. "Emily. Are you at home? Do

you have some orange juice in the fridge? Or some grapes?" She shook her head sharply. "I don't care about Tim and his dang keys. Oh, now, don't cry. We're going to get you some help"—she waved in my direction, signaling that I should get right on that—"but I need you to focus."

I dashed across the work room and grabbed the phone handset off the wall. I had just hit the second "1" in 911 when the alley door crashed open and Alice flew back in.

"Relax, Mom, I just forgot my..." She trailed off as she took in the scene in the kitchen, Bree grim-faced and speaking earnestly into Alice's cell and me dancing from foot to foot with the landline receiver to my ear.

"Nine-one-one. What's the nature of your emergency?" I recognized Vonda Hudson's three-pack-a-day growl.

"Vonda, this is Tally Jones. We need an ambulance for a woman named Emily Clowper. She's a diabetic, and I think something's real wrong with her."

Out of the corner of my eye, I saw Alice sag a little, but in a heartbeat she was at my side.

"Tally? You at home or at the A-la-mode?"

"What?" It took me a second to figure out why Vonda was asking where I was. "No, Emily's not here. Bree's got her on the phone. She's at her own house, I think. But I don't know the address."

Alice snatched the phone from my hand.

"Dr. Clowper lives on Sagebrush, between Ford and Hillcrest," she said, her voice clear and precise. I felt a pang of shame that our little girl had a better handle on this crisis than I did.

"I don't know the street number," she continued, "but it's on the, uh"—she closed her eyes, and lids fluttered faintly as she thought—"I think it's the north side of the street. About halfway down the block, a yellow house with a wide porch and two live oaks in the front yard."

"Emily? Emily!" Bree yelled into the cell phone. "Emily, honey, you need to stay awake and talk to me."

Alice hung up the landline. She sidled up close to me and took my hand, laced her fingers through mine and squeezed tight. Together, we watched Bree trying to talk Emily back from the brink.

"Emily, are you there? Tell me more about the keys and the money." Finally, Bree looked up, her expression stricken. "She's not talking anymore," she murmured. "I think I can hear her breathing, but she's not talking." After another moment, Bree cursed softly. "She hung up."

"What do we do, Mom?"

Those little words, in Alice's tiny voice, brought Bree to her senses. She stood up straight, renewed purpose in her eyes. "Tally, get the keys. We're going to go find Emily."

Fifteen

With Alice navigating, we managed to beat the ambulance to Emily's house.

Alice tumbled out of the van and raced across the lawn, took the porch steps in a single leap, and had her hand on the doorknob before Bree could yell, "Stop!"

Something in that maternal command cut through Alice's panic and she froze long enough for me and Bree to catch up to her.

"You two wait here," I said. "Flag down the ambulance. Call Finn."

Alice appeared torn, but her fear got the better of her and she sagged against her mother's side. Bree nodded, and I tried the door.

Open.

Emily's front door opened into her living room. Her house seemed to be about the same vintage as ours, but without our family's clutter, it appeared strangely sterile and cold. A low green velvet sofa, sagging in the middle, and a single bentwood rocker were the only furnishings.

I knew Emily had been teaching at Dickerson for five years, but it looked like she'd just moved in.

"Emily?" My voice echoed off the whitewashed plank walls and oak floors.

One side of the living room opened onto a dining room and

then a kitchen. The lights were on in both rooms, and I didn't see Emily, so I made a beeline down the hallway that led off the living room, opening doors as I went. First, an empty bedroom, littered with open boxes of books but no furniture. Then an immaculate bathroom that smelled strongly of bleach.

At the end of the hallway, right next to an archway leading into the kitchen, a final door was pulled to but not latched.

"Emily?" I called as I pushed the door open.

"Oh, God."

A lamp sitting on the bare wood floor, its shade draped with a red scarf, cast hellish light and shadow over the scene. Emily sat sprawl-legged atop her brass bed, her body canted forward like a broken doll. Something, it looked like the belt to a bathrobe, stretched between her neck and the brass headboard.

I rushed to her side, and tried to shift her body to reduce the tension in the makeshift noose, but I couldn't get any leverage from the slippery oak floors. Wedging my knee in the fluffy duvet didn't help.

My fingers grasped at the slip knot around her neck, and then at the more substantial knot on the headboard, but the weight of Emily's body pulled the fabric tight.

Frantic, I dashed out of the bedroom and into the kitchen, desperate to find a knife or scissors.

No clutter in the kitchen, either. A butcher-block island in the middle of the room had a cell phone and a gold foil take-out box on top. The take-out box was open, a fork resting half in and half out of the box, and I saw a perfect square of tiramisu nestled inside. Other than the forgotten snack and the phone, though, the counters were bare.

I yanked open the first drawer I found, but it was stuffed with receipts, half-used birthday candles, and plastic packets of soy sauce. The next drawer held cutlery, but nothing sharper than a butter knife.

Finally, I found a paring knife wedged behind rolls of plastic wrap and boxes of sandwich bags.

I raced back into the bedroom and started sawing on the bathrobe tie, but the paring knife didn't have much of an edge.

My breath came in heaving sobs and I found myself cursing everything under the sun—the knife, the bathrobe tie, Emily herself, my wimpy arms, everything. I tried not to notice how still Emily was, without even the faint stirring of breath in her body. At last I heard the clatter and commotion of emergency personnel from the front room.

"We're back here," I screamed.

I didn't drop the knife until a paramedic pried my hand loose and pulled me bodily from the bed. Tears blurring my vision, I watched the medics cut Emily loose with a single movement, lift her off the bed, and begin CPR.

I backed out of the bedroom, then turned and ran out of the house. Outside, the once-quiet street swarmed with rescue vehicles—an ambulance, two fire trucks, and a half-dozen cop cars. Cal physically restrained Finn Harper, who seemed determined to get to Emily's side. It seemed all of Dalliance had descended on Emily's tiny yellow house in response to the call for help, and yet I knew that effort would not be enough.

I knew Emily Clowper was dead.

Bree held a weeping Alice in her arms, and I took hold of Finn's hand and held it tight, all of us standing just outside the circle of flashing red lights, while Cal waded into the swarm of first responders to find out what happened.

We didn't have to wait for Cal's report to know that Emily had passed. We watched in horror as the paramedics wheeled an empty stretcher out of her house, loaded it into the ambulance, and drove away with their sirens silent. They'd left Emily in the care of the police.

"Obviously, there will be an investigation," Cal said when

he returned. "But it looks pretty cut and dried. By all appearances, Emily Clowper gave in and took her own life."

Finn took a step toward Cal, and I laid a restraining hand on his arm. "'Gave in'? What are you implying?"

"I'm not implying anything, Finn. I'm saying that Dr. Clowper was going through a lot these days, and some people can't handle stress well."

Finn shook off my hand. "And whose fault is that, Cal? You and your henchmen were breathing down her neck. Forced the university to put her on leave. Had the whole town pointing at her with suspicion."

"Look, Finn. I'm not going to debate you here and now. I'm just telling you the facts as they appear at the moment. There'll be plenty of time to point the finger of blame later."

"It's my fault," Alice cried. "I turned on her when she needed me."

Bree tutted softly and pressed Alice's face to her breast. "No, sugar, this isn't your fault."

Finn leaned over as though he'd been punched in the gut, rested his hands on his knees and groaned. "God, if this is anyone's fault, it's mine. Emily and I have been friends for ten years, and I all but called her a whore tonight."

Cal watched the wailing and gnashing of teeth impassively, a raised eyebrow his only indication of surprise.

"Huh," he said. "You mind telling me what the hell happened tonight? I thought you all were thick as thieves."

I pulled him aside and filled him in on the evening's revelations.

"Huh," he said.

"That's it? 'Huh'?"

"Just give me a minute, okay?" Cal rubbed the back of his neck. "So you were the last person to see her at the A-la-mode?"

I nodded.

"What did you two talk about after everyone left? How did she seem?"

"How do you think? She was sad. Embarrassed by her affair. Worried about her job. Upset that she'd disappointed so many people."

"How upset?"

"If you're asking whether she seemed despondent, like someone about to take her own life, the answer is 'no.' But..." I glanced over at Finn and Alice, both wrapped up in misery and guilt. More than anything, I didn't want them to bear the burden of believing their fight with Emily pushed her to suicide.

"But what?" Cal prompted.

I looked up at him, at the unforgiving geometry of his face and the clear light of certainty in his eyes.

I'm not a perfect person. In fact, I've done a lot of stupid things, and even a few mean ones, in my time. But I don't lie. I knew what lies did to people. When my mama found out about my daddy's other family up in Tulsa, it killed her. Her body lived on for years, but her soul was as dead as could be. Lies hurt.

This time, the truth might hurt, too. But I had to tell it.

"Right before she left, she said it would be okay. That she thought she knew what she had to do to make everything better."

Cal nodded. "I sure hope she didn't think suicide was gonna fix things. Because that"—he pointed at Finn and Alice, holding each other for comfort—"that sure doesn't look like 'okay' to me."

Sixteen

Finn followed me, Bree, and Alice home. He brewed a pot of herbal tea while I dug out a package of the high-end chocolate chip cookies that had been hidden in the cabinet above the fridge so they stood a chance of surviving until we had company.

When we'd gathered in the living room, we all just stared at the plate of cookies. Even the promise of extra-large chunks of chocolate and macadamia nuts held little appeal.

"Does she have family?" Bree asked.

Finn nodded. "Her folks are in Duluth. Cal said the police will call them tonight, but I'll call them in the morning. I can help them make arrangements, but I bet they'll want to..."

His voice grew tight, then trailed off. I knew what he was thinking—that her family would want to take her home to bury her—but it didn't seem right to say the words out loud. We'd all just seen Emily, spoken with her, argued with her. To talk about that person we knew as just a body to be buried, felt too sudden, too final.

"Duluth?" Bree said. "Poor kid. She was pretty far from home."

Finn shrugged. "Most academics don't get a choice. You graduate and you go wherever you get a job."

I remembered what Emily had said about the two body problem, and the difficulty of married academics finding jobs in the same state, let alone the same city.

"Emily always knew she might end up someplace far from Minnesota," Finn said, "call some new place 'home.'"

Still, I thought of her sparsely furnished house, her dogless life, and my heart broke. Some people, when they move to a new town, they make a new home there. Emily had not. She had been in Dalliance for years, but was clearly still a stranger.

"We should do something here, too," Alice said. "We—"

She broke off, her whole body wracked with sobs. Bree pulled her close, enveloping her in a fierce hug. "It's okay, baby. We'll say good-bye to her."

I glanced at Finn. His eyes swam with tears as he watched mother and daughter grieve. But then he shook himself, physically casting off the raw emotion of the moment.

Cal and Finn thought of each other as oil and water, but they were really two sides of the same coin. Emily had pointed out that Finn shared Cal's deep sense of integrity, but where Cal followed the rules, Finn made his own. And both men shied away from sorrow, Cal falling back on action and Finn falling back on intellect.

I didn't know the man Finn Harper had become, but I knew the boy he'd been. And that boy would treat his loss as a puzzle to be solved, while the hurt he felt simmered beneath the surface, eating at his soul.

"Tally, how did Emily seem when she left the store last night?" Finn asked.

I weighed my options, considered shrugging off the question, and decided on full disclosure. I repeated the story I'd told Cal, about Emily's last words to me.

But Finn didn't interpret them the same way Cal did. "I got the sense that a lightbulb had gone off for her when we were arguing, but I was too angry then to listen. Maybe she had an idea about who killed Bryan."

"Oh, man. If she did, maybe that's why she called. To tell

me what she'd figured out. I can't believe I didn't have my phone when she called," Alice said, pushing herself out of her mother's arms. The child was bound and determined to make this her fault.

"Sweetie, it wouldn't have mattered," Bree said. "She was already in a bad way when she called. She didn't make any sense at all."

"Was she drunk?" Alice asked.

"I doubt it," Finn said. "Because of her medical condition, she didn't drink. Even if she were upset, there wouldn't have been alcohol in the house. My guess is she took too much insulin. That would have sent her blood sugar plummeting and left her dopey, confused, and weak."

"She seemed so on top of her illness, though," I said. "How could she take too much insulin unless it was on purpose?"

Finn shrugged. "It happened once when we were dating. She uses"—he cringed—"used both long- and short-acting insulin. The long-acting stuff she took morning and evening, like clockwork. The short-acting insulin was for regulating her sugar after eating an unusually big meal. It packs a punch. One morning, she was tired and she accidentally picked up the vial of short-acting insulin. She bottomed out fast and had to drink some juice right away."

"I told her to get some OJ or some fruit," Bree said. "I remembered that from Steel Magnolias, when Julia Roberts got all wonky in the beauty parlor. But from what she said, she was in bed. She said she was too tired to go to the kitchen."

"What else did she say?" Finn asked. "I mean, if she was having a crisis with her insulin, why would she call Alice instead of 911?"

Bree shook her head and her cheeks turned almost as red as her hair. "I don't really know. Like I said, she wasn't making any sense."

"Come on, Mom. Just tell us what she said. Maybe it will make sense to one of us."

"Well, she asked for Alice, and I told her Alice had left for the evening. Then she said she had to lay down and that her bed was really soft. I said Alice had to sleep, too, but she said she needed to talk to Alice, it was important, Alice was brilliant. Then she said something like, 'What she said. Keys. Tim.'"

"Huh?" I asked.

"Like I said, it didn't make any sense. And she was whispering. It was hard to understand her, but I'm almost one hundred percent certain that's what she said. I asked her who Tim was and what keys he had, but she just said, 'No! Keys. Tim. Money.'" Bree swallowed hard. "And then she asked for candy. That's when your Aunt Tally figured out what was going on." Bree grabbed Alice's hand and held it tight. "I'm so sorry. I didn't know she was sick."

I held my breath, terrified Alice would snap at her mother and break Bree's heart. But, instead, she squeezed her mom's hand and offered her a wobbly smile.

Finn finally gave in to the lure of the cookies. He took a bite and chewed thoughtfully. "So Alice is brilliant. Keys, Tim, and money. What could it mean?"

"I have her keys," Alice said, "but I don't know anyone named Tim. Except for Timmy Jenkins, that kid who lived next door to us when we lived in San Antonio. But no one named Tim at school."

Finn sighed. "It might not mean anything at all," he said. "Since my mom had her stroke, she's had some bad episodes where she starts talking about all sorts of gibberish. The doctor told me that when the brain is starving, random synapses fire. Mom's brain gets starved for oxygen, but I bet if Emily's brain was starved for sugar it would do the same thing. We may be looking for meaning where none exists."

Bree looked like something was eating her up inside, but every time she opened her mouth like she was ready to talk, she'd glance at her daughter and stop.

"Alice, honey," I said gently, "you've had quite a day. Why don't you try to get some rest?"

The mere suggestion of sleep triggered a yawn, which Alice fought to smother. "No way. I know how this works. You send me off to bed, and then you talk about what's really going on. But I think I deserve to be a part of this conversation, don't you? She was my teacher, my friend."

Bree and I exchanged a look, but we both knew Alice was right. She'd earned her seat at the grown-up table the hard way.

"What's bugging you, Bree?" I asked.

"It may be nothing, but I would swear I heard a voice in the background when she called. It was muffled, and I couldn't make out any words." She shook her head in frustration. "I don't know, maybe it was the television. Or maybe it was the power of suggestion. I had just learned she had a fu-, um, a boyfriend and so maybe I imagined she had late-night company. But I don't think so."

Bree looked around at each of us in turn, her expression earnest.

"I think someone else was in Emily's house tonight. I think she was whispering because she didn't want someone to hear her on the phone."

I nodded. "Normally, I'd say you were nuttier than a scoop of praline pecan, but I think you may be right."

Finn leaned forward, his cookie forgotten. "All right, Nancy Drew. Lay it on me," he said.

I told them what I'd found in the kitchen, the gold take-out box of tiramisu and the fork.

"She loved tiramisu, right?" A look of pain flashed across Finn's face as he nodded. "That was the one thing she couldn't resist, even though she wasn't supposed to eat dessert. If she were going to kill herself, do you think she would have passed up one last opportunity to indulge?"

Out loud, it sounded weak. But after the conversation Emily and I had about denying ourselves pleasure and putting off happiness, I found it hard to imagine that she would have passed up the opportunity for a little indulgence.

Finn picked up the thread of my argument. "Leaving aside the armchair psychology, where did the dessert come from? Em and I had dinner together last night. We went to Café Siam. No tiramisu on the menu there. And then we went directly to the A-la-mode, and she left there way too late to hit a restaurant for dessert. If she'd gotten the tiramisu earlier during the day or on Thursday, why would it have been on the counter instead of in the fridge?"

From the expression on her face, Alice had her thinking hat on.

"There's no way she killed herself," she said. "Mom, you said she was slurring her words and talking about laying down, right?" Bree nodded. "Well, if Dr. Clowper's blood sugar was so low that she couldn't even talk right and she was calling from the bedroom, how did she get the phone back to the kitchen?"

Finn nodded. "For that matter, how did she manage to..." His voice trailed off and he threw a nervous look at Alice.

"It's okay, Mr. Harper. I know what you're getting at. How did she manage to tie the knots and strangle herself when she was basically incoherent?"

We all sat mulling that over for a minute. Finally, Finn broke the silence.

"Shit. She was murdered, wasn't she?"

Bree and I nodded tentatively, but Alice showed more commitment. "I can picture exactly what happened. Someone, someone she knew, was in her house. That person managed to get her to take too much insulin, or the wrong kind of insulin. Then, when she was too weak to fight back, that person strangled her, making it look like suicide."

It sent chills down my spine to have our sweet Alice describe the particulars of murder with such clinical precision, but she painted a compelling picture.

Alice leaned forward earnestly. "Whatever she'd figured out about Bryan's death," she said, "it got her killed."

"And whatever she'd figured out," Bree said to her child, her voice tight with emotion, "she thought you had the answer."

"But I don't have any idea what she was talking about," Alice said.

"Shit," Finn said again. "It doesn't matter what you know or don't know, Alice. Emily said you held the key, and her murderer was probably standing right there when she said it."

Seventeen

By morning, news of Emily Clowper's death had spread clear across Lantana County. The official cause of death might take weeks, but the preliminary statement by the coroner's office was that Emily had died from self-inflicted asphyxiation.

Somehow the staff at the *News-Letter* had taken that informal conclusion and cobbled together a brief story for the Saturday morning edition, throwing in a few seemingly offhanded references to Emily's connection to the recent murder of Bryan Campbell. The innuendo led to the obvious conclusion that guilt drove Emily to despair. It seemed impossible to imagine that her suicide and Bryan's murder weren't somehow connected, especially when linking them created such a neat TV movie story line.

And that sort of storybook closure made for better PR—for the Dalliance PD, the Chamber of Commerce, and Dickerson University—than the notion of a killer on the loose.

Bree spent the whole day mulling over the fact that Emily had probably been murdered over some kernel of information her daughter possessed. She got more and more torqued up as the day progressed, until finally she exploded.

"No way in hell are you spending one minute more than you have to on that campus."

We were sitting at the kitchen table, wolfing down plates of leftover meatloaf and mashed potatoes while Kyle watched the

A-la-mode during the dinner hour lull. Alice carefully mounded a dab of potato on top of a tiny square of meatloaf and levered the perfect mouthful onto her fork.

"No problem. Once the May term starts on Wednesday, I'll only have to be on campus for the three hours of class in the morning and maybe for another hour of so afterwards, for helping students and meeting with Reggie. I can do my grading at home."

"Nuh-uh," Bree said. "I mean it. You're not going to campus. You just tell that Reggie person you've changed your mind and you can't help him with that class."

"Mama—"

"Don't 'Mama' me, Alice Marie Anders. Unless you turned eighteen when I wasn't looking, you still gotta do as I say, and I say you're not stepping foot on the Dickerson campus until they catch this murderer."

"Why not?"

Bree rolled her eyes. "I musta dropped you on your pointy head one too many times. Two people are dead already, and you're smack in the middle of the trouble. It's not safe for you to be on campus."

Alice tipped her head in that calculating way she had, all cold logic to Bree's fiery emotion. "Dr. Clowper wasn't on campus when she was murdered. If someone wants me dead, they'll find me."

Her words found their mark, and all the color drained from Bree's face. She couldn't shelter her child from danger; no place was safe. Her breath hitched audibly, and I thought she might start to hyperventilate.

"At least if I'm on campus," Alice continued, "there will be lots of people around. I'll probably be safer there than, say, the alley behind Remember the A-la-mode."

Bree rolled her lips between her teeth and squinted hard at

her troublesome child. I swallowed a groan, because I knew that look. Alice came by her smarts honestly, and she got them from her mother. When Bree gave up the footloose and fancy-free persona and got down to business, she was a formidable opponent for her genius child.

"I don't like it," Bree muttered.

Alice reached out to pat her mother's hand. "I know you don't like it, Mama, but I can't back out on my obligation. I'll be okay."

"Yes, you will. Because I'm not letting you out of my sight."

"Mama—"

"Save your breath, little girl. I know you want to TA this class. So I'll just go with you."

"Mom!" Alice shrieked, all horrified teenager. Her fork clattered to her plate.

"It's not open for discussion."

"You can't just follow me to class."

"Watch me."

"No, really, you can't. The school has a policy against people sitting in on classes unless they're registered. They don't want people getting an education they haven't paid for."

Mother and daughter faced off across the remains of our family meal, each sizing up the other, looking for tells, any indication that the other was bluffing. They could have given lessons on brinksmanship to Cold War-era diplomats.

"Fine," Bree conceded. "I'll register for the class. American Literature, right?"

Alice snorted.

"What? I may talk like I got a banjo up my ass, but I can read, you know," Bree drawled.

"You can't just register for a class like that." Alice snapped her fingers. "Dickerson is a selective school."

Check.

Bree's eyes lit with triumph. "But they have that community outreach program for folks who aren't getting a degree. Vonda Hudson took a class on art history before she took that trip to Italy, and she's a lovely woman but she's dumb as a box of hair."

"But Vonda has a high school diploma," Alice countered. And you don't. Alice didn't say the words, but they echoed in the silence anyway.

Checkmate.

The stricken pain in Bree's eyes was so raw I had to look away. A flicker of uncertainty, maybe a little shame, flashed across Alice's face before she stuck out her jaw in resolve.

Bree made out how she was a party girl and pretended to be a screwup in school, but she actually got really good grades in high school. A pregnancy scare forced her to drop out and get married. In the end, she lost that baby along with her dreams of getting out of Dalliance, going someplace where she could shed her hell-raising reputation and make something of herself. She talked a good game, but her lack of an education shamed her.

I watched as she got a grip on her emotions and straightened her spine. She reached out for the bowl of mashed potatoes and spooned up another serving onto her plate.

"Fair enough. I didn't graduate from high school, but your Aunt Tally did."

"What?" I piped up, not sure how I got dragged into this spat.

"Aunt Tally can register for the class and go with you every day. She's already told Reggie Hawking that she's interested in going back to school"—she paused to give me a pointed look, reminding me that I owed her big for helping Alice search through Bryan's office—"so it shouldn't surprise anyone when she registers for the class."

"Now wait a minute," I protested. "I have a business to run. I already applied for a permit for a booth at the Bluegrass

Festival, and now I've got this benefit for Bryan Campbell to plan, not to mention Crystal Tompkins's wedding. It's going to be a busy summer."

Bree turned the full force of her glare on me, and all the good reasons why I shouldn't go back to college that summer melted away like soft serve in the sunlight.

After we put away the dishes and refilled Sherbet's kibble dish, we headed back to the A-la-mode.

"Y'all go ahead," I said. "I'll be right there."

Once Bree and Alice were out of earshot, I pulled my phone out of my purse and dialed.

I got voice mail, and said a little "thank you" for that bit of luck.

"Hey, Cal," I said to the machine. "Tally here. Uh, I want to be straight with you, okay? This is my official notice. I'm fixin' to meddle."

Eighteen

Bree promised she would take care of the A-la-mode while I embarked on my new career as a part-time college student, and she honored her word. She headed out the door at five a.m. Monday morning, her flaming curls tied in a sloppy top knot and a travel mug of lukewarm day-old coffee clutched to her breast like a long-lost lover. As she shoved out the door, she speared me with an accusatory finger: "Register. Today."

I did as I was told, schlepping down to the Dickerson Registrar's Office. Thankfully, the school played fast and loose with registration for community members who weren't seeking a degree. If you were willing to pay the tuition, they'd let you register.

My hand shook as I wrote the check. After nine months, the A-la-mode had finally drifted into the black, and I had money in my checking account. But not much. As I scrawled the zeros on the tuition check, I couldn't help but envision all the things I wouldn't be buying for another few months. The professional sign to replace the one Bree and Alice had painted freehand. The new waffle cone press I coveted. The brake job for my wretched old van.

But family came first.

First and second, as it happened.

After I got myself officially enrolled in Reggie Hawking's American Lit class, I met Cal by the entrance to the Gish-Tunny

Center. He'd set up a meeting with Jonas Landry and George Gunderson to discuss the benefit for Bryan's scholarship.

Before we got down to the specifics of the party, though, Cal decided to take me to the woodshed.

"Dammit, Tally, what sort of nonsense are you and Bree cooking up now?"

"It's not nonsense, Cal." I explained our logic about why we thought Emily had been murdered. "If someone killed both Bryan and Emily and if that someone thinks Alice is a threat, she's in danger. I'm not about to sit by and let someone hurt our baby."

"Those are some mighty big 'ifs,'" Cal said.

"Maybe. But it's mighty big trouble if we're right."

He sighed. "Listen, I would ride you more about this, but there's nothing left for you to meddle in. It's not official, but it looks like the detectives are closing the book on Bryan's murder and there won't be much of an investigation into Emily's suicide."

I noticed he didn't qualify that word at all. As far as Cal and the cops were concerned, Emily definitely killed herself.

"If there's no official investigation," he continued, "there's nothing for you to muck up. You may be a busybody, but you're not a criminal."

"Gee, thanks," I said.

He tipped an imaginary hat. "No problem, darlin'."

The two professors joined us as we picked up paper cups of sweet tea from the Jump and Java. They both bought coffee, waving their identification cards in front of the little red eye the way Reggie had done, and then they led us up to the third floor ballroom.

"This is the space," Landry said. "We can drape the whole room in crimson and gold bunting, and we have a parquet dance floor we can lay over the carpet there."

The room stretched before us, empty and a bit forlorn, but with the enormous crystal chandeliers blazing and the space softened with furniture, fabric, and music, I could imagine how lovely it would be.

Cal nodded. "We're planning on a silent auction," he said, "so we could set up the items along that wall."

I piped up. "Deena Silver is pretty busy with her daughter's wedding, but Crystal and Jason knew Bryan, so she's willing to do the catering at cost as long as we don't hold the event the weekend of the wedding, which is the third weekend in June. And I'd like to provide dessert, if that's okay. Since it's a more formal dinner, I thought I could do an ice cream cake."

A faint smile graced Cal's lips. "That would be just fine, Tally. Since Bryan came to Dickerson, he's been focused on the finer things, but when he was a kid, he had an ice cream cake from the Tasty-Swirl for every birthday party."

He cleared his throat. "So how's the second weekend in June look? That would work with the college baseball season and still leave Deena free the weekend of Crystal's wedding."

Landry pulled a face. "Unfortunately, I'll be away that weekend. I have to attend the IAFS conference in Vancouver." He looked at me. "Sorry, that's the International Association of Film Scholarship."

"Is it official, then?" Gunderson asked.

Landry chuckled. "As of Friday. I indulged in the osso buco at Fra Cirilo to celebrate."

Gunderson explained. "Jonas's most recent book was nominated for the IAFS Tamke Award, their highest honor. It seems he's won."

"Congratulations," Cal and I said.

It must have been a big deal to rate a dinner at Fra Cirilo, North Texas's poshest Italian restaurant.

"Yes, well, it means I'll have to miss the benefit. What a

disappointment."

Maybe I was projecting my own lack of enthusiasm onto Jonas Landry, but he didn't sound disappointed at all. In fact, I thought I detected a note of relief in his voice, like he was downright delighted to have an excuse not to attend the benefit.

"Nonsense," Cal said. "We couldn't have this event without you there. We'll just have to move it up a week."

I smothered a curse. Did these men have any idea what this event would involve? I could already imagine the stream of profanity spewing from Deena's mouth when I informed her that we had less than a month to plan this shindig. And now that I would be trying to balance the A-la-mode and this literature class along with the preparations...just thinking about it made me tired.

That evening, after a day spent running errands, I found a package on my doorstep, a flat rectangle wrapped in brown paper and tied with a big, sloppy pink bow. Were it not for the pink bow, I might have thought it was a bomb, but the pink bow gave me hope it was a real live present.

And it was. Of sorts.

I sat on the couch, carefully pulled the ribbon off, and then ripped through the paper and found a book.

I like books. I like to read mysteries and romances, cookbooks and the occasional biography. But I never had much of an inkling to read Disciple of Denmark: The Life and Filmography of Christer Rasmussen, by Jonas Landry, which was—I flipped open the back cover—four hundred seventy-two pages long.

There was a note tucked inside the front cover of the book: "For Tally, I thought you might like to see what all the fuss is about. And then you can tell me—Cal."

Sherbet jumped up beside me and started nibbling at the end of the pink ribbon.

"I don't think so, little man. I am not taking you back to the vet tonight." I tugged the ribbon away and tucked it between the folds of the paper before pulling the cat onto my lap.

"What do you think, Sherbet? In honor of my new status as 'college student' do you think I should tackle this nasty looking book?"

Sherbet squeaked and butted his head on the corner of the hard cover.

"Do you want to do my homework for me, little man?" He squeaked again. "I didn't think so."

I was petting the cat's silky head and idly flipping through the first pages of the book, trying to decide whether etiquette required me to actually read the thing, when a word caught my eye.

It was near the bottom of the third page, just one little word at the beginning of a paragraph, but it rocked my world.

Ostergard.

It creeped me out a little that, as we convened around the back table of the A-la-mode, Kyle took the chair Emily had usually occupied. But it was the seat closest to the wall outlet, and he had his laptop fired up.

I've heard it said that people tend to look like their dogs, and it seemed the same could be said about laptop computers. Where Emily used a sleek white machine, all slim curved lines, Kyle's laptop had a dark case, its clunky frame covered over with stickers for bands and skateboard manufacturers.

"Tally, you don't have Wi-Fi here, do you?" Finn asked.

"Huh?"

Alice laughed, and Kyle snorted. "No," he said. "But McKlesky and Howard does."

"The law firm?"

"Yep."

"Isn't their network password protected?" Finn sounded

incredulous.

"Nope."

"Incredible."

"I know, right?"

Kyle and Finn bumped fists. Apparently their mutual disdain for McKlesky and Howard's idiocy provided some sort of cement for their boy-bonding.

"Ostergard?" Kyle asked.

"That's right. Walder—with a 'd' instead of a 't'—Ostergard."

"Huh."

"Let me see," Alice said, pulling the laptop around in front of her. Kyle held up his hands, seemingly surrendering his machine to her.

She read silently for a second, clicking keys on the computer.

"This must be him," she said. "Walder Ostergard, ASC. Cinematographer. His Wikipedia entry says he's from Denmark but lived in the U.S. for the last thirty years of his life. Died last summer. Worked extensively with Christer Rasmussen before immigrating."

"That's the guy," I said. I scanned through the paragraph in Landry's book, the one that mentioned Ostergard. "Landry thanks him for helping arrange the interviews he did with Rasmussen."

"That's why the book is such a big deal," Alice said. "From what Reggie said, Rasmussen was notoriously reclusive—like J. D. Salinger reclusive. The fact that Landry got to interview him extensively before he died, it's huge."

"But what's fake?" Bree asked. "Wasn't that what Bryan's calendar said? That Ostergard was fake? But he's a real person. Dead, but real."

"I don't know," Alice said. "Maybe there's something in his blog."

"Blog?" Bree asked.

Kyle rolled his eyes. Working with old ladies like us about drove him nuts.

"Blog," he said. "Web log, like an online diary."

"Don't take that tone with me, Kyle Mason," Bree snapped. "What kind of idiot keeps a diary out on the Internet where everyone can read it?"

"Oh, just everyone," Kyle drawled.

"I don't suppose he blogs in English?" Finn said.

"Actually he does," Alice replied. She read silently a moment. "Broken profane English, but English."

Something jogged loose in my brain.

"That's got to be it," I said. "Reggie mentioned that Landry was pissed at Bryan last fall, and he made some comment about Bryan spending too much time reading blogs. Reggie thought Bryan wasn't doing his work, but maybe Landry was upset over something Bryan found on a blog."

I felt a growing certainty that this was it, the key to everything. In my experience, when people cheated on their spouses they displayed a fundamental lack of character, a failing that spilled into other aspects of their lives. If Jonas Landry could cheat so boldly, what else might he do? Lie? Kill?

Still, my innate dislike for Jonas Landry wouldn't get us far in a court of law. If Jonas killed Bryan, we'd have to unravel the whole story, start to finish.

Alice moaned. "But what?" she said, echoing my own thoughts. "What did Bryan find? Jeez, if it's something on Ostergard's blog, we're doomed. The guy may not have spoken English very well, but he sure liked to write. It looks like he averaged a good twenty posts a month, and the index goes back for years."

"I've got it," Finn said. "I'm taking my mom to the hospital for some tests tomorrow. It'll take all day. So just give me the

URL for the blog and the book, and I'll see what I can figure out."

Nineteen

I was an average student in high school, earning mostly As and Bs through hard work rather than native brilliance. I probably could have gotten into college, but I had no way to pay tuition. Mama and I had to pinch pennies till they squealed just to get by. My daddy had a whole other family to support up in Tulsa, and I sure wasn't in a position to win scholarships. Heck, even if I'd been able to find the cash, I couldn't have gone far: my mama needed constant supervision when she was drinking. Which was always.

Bottom line, college simply wasn't an option.

As a result, most of what I knew about universities I'd learned from watching television. I expected the offices of the faculty to be grand affairs with wood paneling, floor to ceiling bookshelves, and tall, leaded-glass windows. Lecture halls should be filled with oak desks, a stately podium at the front of the room, golden sunlight streaming through ivy-draped windows, and the scent of leather-bound books heavy on the air. The outside of Dickerson, and even the big public atrium in Sinclair Hall, fit my Hollywood image of a private university. But once you peeled back that top layer and got down to the real working part of the school, the image shattered.

When I crossed the threshold into the main lecture hall in Sinclair Hall, the fusty scent of lunch meat and damp socks hit me hard.

Buzzing fluorescent tubes cast unforgiving light on the chipped laminate desks bolted into a tiered floor covered in stained commercial carpet. The chairs, too, were bolted in place, their hard, plastic contours splattered with Magic Marker graffiti. The walls of the room were covered with a chaos of posters for study abroad programs, sorority fund-raisers, and summer subletting opportunities.

At the front of the room, Reggie stood beside a lectern resting on an office desk. Behind him, a vast whiteboard bore the ghostly marks of lectures past. He glanced up and gave me a quick smile before returning to studying the black binder in his hands.

I spotted Alice sitting in the front right corner of the classroom, narrow shoulders squared beneath a baby blue cardigan, a half-dozen sharpened pencils and two highlighters lined up next to an open notebook on the table in front of her.

I made my way toward the middle of the classroom, wanting to be close enough to Alice to keep an eye on her but not so close as to make her self-conscious. I found a seat about five rows from the front and only a few in from the aisle. As I settled in, I could tell that even my ample behind would be no match for a full three hours in that hard plastic seat.

"Hey, mama."

I craned my neck around to see the boy who had spoken, a thick-necked young man with Greek letters emblazoned across his chest, knee-length khaki shorts, and leather flip-flops. The sort of flip-flops that cost more than my best dress shoes. He wore a puka shell necklace, a backward ball cap, and sprawled in his chair, slumped down so far his butt about fell off the edge of his seat.

I hadn't gone to college, but I knew his type. I'd wrangled boys like that when I worked at Erma's Fry By Night Diner in high school, the rich kids from Dickerson who had more money than manners. I'd watched those boys grow into men with florid faces, sports cars, and inappropriate girlfriends. And I'd watched those men grow fat and sad with middle age, turning into pitiful caricatures of themselves. Basically, I'd watched the life cycle of this boy's type, and I would bet he wouldn't be smiling such a smug grin if he knew what was in store for him.

A half dozen smirking boys formed a gangly knot around the boy who'd spoken. This particular breed of jerk tended to travel in packs.

"I haven't seen you around campus," he said, undeterred by my most thin-lipped glare of annoyance. "You new? Cuz maybe I could, uh, show you around." He bobbled his eyebrows suggestively, and his posse sniggered.

The ringleader high-fived the kid next to him and laughed, but the sound had an ugly edge to it. Whether he ever pantsed a kid in gym class or not, this guy was a bully.

As a girl from the wrong side of the tracks, I'd learned that the best way to beat a bully is to ignore him. I swiveled back around, prepared to do just that, but my rebuff only prompted a round of catcalls from the peanut gallery.

I swung back around. "Sugar, I'm old enough to be your mama, so don't think your cute will work on me."

"Meow," he said, swiping a playful claw through the air. "A real live cougar!" His backup bullies laughed way louder than his comment deserved.

I opened my mouth to put him in his place, but before I could utter a word, someone behind me came to my defense.

"Put it back in your pants, Bubba. She doesn't have time for your bull crap."

I turned around to thank my champion, and found Ashley Henderson, the perky desk clerk from the Lady Shapers, a high-end all-girl fitness club in town. I'd done a little undercover work—emphasis on the "little" instead of the "work"—there the year before, and Ashley had inadvertently given me some very useful information. Given how transparent middle-aged women were to vivacious young girls like her, I couldn't imagine she would remember me, but she surprised me.

"Hey, Miz Jones," she said.

"Hey, Ashley. Thanks for that."

She waved her hand dismissively. "Bubba's a jackass. You get used to him."

Her words were friendly enough, to me if not to Bubba, but her shuttered expression and flat tone of voice did not invite girl talk. "Well, thanks anyway," I said.

She nodded and turned to her notebook. I flipped open my own, and mindlessly jotted the date on the top of the page, and then I studied Ashley out of the corner of my eye.

When I'd seen her six months earlier, she'd been as sweet and bubbly as strawberry soda, her highlighted blonde hair caught in a high ponytail and her tight athletic clothes showing off the compact curves of her muscular body.

She'd changed.

Like many Texans, she'd lost her sun-kissed glow during the winter months, but her skin had gone beyond pale to the flat, sallow color of cooked custard. She still wore her hair in a ponytail, but it listed to the side and strands escaped to create a nimbus around her head. The precious matching spandex-enriched cotton outfits she wore to the gym were gone; in their place, she sported a pair of real sweatpants, their original color faded to an indeterminate muddy hue, and an oversized pink sweatshirt with purple Greek letters appliquéd across the chest.

I wasn't judging the girl. Heck, I wasn't dressed much better, and she'd probably been out painting the town the night before. It just surprised me to see her looking so, well, ordinary.

"Ladies and gentlemen," Reggie announced from the front of the classroom. "It's time for us to begin."

And with that, I began my very first and probably last college class.

After an hour and a half of Reggie droning on about the significance of classical liberal political philosophy in the early American novel, I understood why college kids drank coffee all dang day. When he finally announced that we'd take a ten minute break, I grabbed Alice's hand and pulled her bodily out of the classroom and down to the basement where the vending machines hummed contentedly.

"Are you having fun?" Alice asked, as I dug quarters out of my purse for the soda machine.

I searched her face for any hint of sarcasm, found none, and sighed. "Darlin', your Aunt Tally probably isn't cut out for college. Now, your mama might get a kick out of this, but I'd really rather be at home watching ShopNet."

Alice rolled her eyes. "How can you watch that crap? You don't even buy anything. It's weird."

I shrugged as I studied the pictures of different flavors of soda. I couldn't remember which brands of root beer had caffeine and which ones didn't. Unwilling to risk a decaffeinated beverage, I opted for the diet cola.

"I just like looking at the stuff." The can fell into the receptacle at the bottom with a satisfying clunk. "I don't know why. And it's relaxing."

She shivered dramatically. "Hardly."

I'd always had problems with insomnia, with my brain running on overdrive whenever I closed my eyes. Years before, I'd discovered that home shopping channels provided the perfect antidote: just enough sense to keep my mind from flying in a million different directions, but not enough meaning to actually keep me engaged and awake. After enough nights falling asleep to the patter of ShopNet announcers, I'd started to find them soothing even when I was awake. Alice and Bree both thought I should be committed for watching that drivel, but in the grand scheme of vices, bad TV was pretty far down on the list.

I cracked open the can and took a long pull, then had to stifle a little belch. "You want one?" I asked Alice.

"No, thanks."

We'd turned to head to the stairs, Alice leading the way, when we ran into Ashley on her way to the machines. She looked a little unsteady, like maybe she was still a little tipsy from the night before.

"Hi Ashley," Alice said.

"Nnngh," Ashley moaned. She lurched past us, swiped her ID card through the reader built into the machine, and drew out a can of ginger ale.

Poor kid.

I shooed Alice away so Ashley could nurse her hangover in peace.

Even though my mama drank her way to an early grave, I didn't have a problem with partying. Bree and I had both imbibed. Especially Bree. As long as you could say "no," and you didn't put yourself in harm's way, I didn't judge. But Bree called her daughter "Saint Alice" for a reason: we loved her to itty bitty pieces, but she was a prig.

"That's not the best way to start the semester," Alice muttered as we hiked up the stairs.

"What? Ashley?"

"Mmmm-hmmm. We're going to go through this material fast, so if she falls behind..." She shook her head and clucked like an old school marm.

"Lighten up, Alice. For all you know, Ashley's already gotten ahead on the reading and will ace all the tests."

Alice huffed in disbelief. "Right. If she's not careful, she'll fail this class again."

"Again?"

Alice peeked over her shoulder to make sure we were alone. "Yeah, she took this class last fall. From what I heard, she blew it off all semester and then whined her way into an incomplete."

"A what?"

"An incomplete. It's a grade. If you get sick or something at the end of a semester, after the deadline to drop a class, you can request an incomplete. You just have to finish up the work the next term, and then the grade gets changed to whatever you earned."

"Was Ashley sick?" I asked with surprise. The girl I'd seen near the end of last October seemed the very picture of health.

Alice rolled her eyes. "No, she just got all weepy and said that she was broken up over Brittanie Brinkman dying, since they were sorority sisters and all."

Now it was my turn to scoff. I talked with Ashley just after Brittanie was murdered, and I knew for a fact that Ashley despised Brittanie and didn't care a lick about the other girl's death.

"I know, right? Anyway, she got her incomplete from Bryan. Grade changes were due the week before Spring finals—I walked a couple of the forms over to the Registrar's Office for Dr. Clowper—and I'm guessing Ashley must have failed, because otherwise she wouldn't be here today."

We reached the top of the stairs, and Alice glanced at her phone to check the time. "We've still got a few minutes. Let's get some sun."

Together, we pushed through the back doors of Sinclair and found ourselves on a little patio, ringed by iron benches and delicate crepe myrtles, aflame with fuchsia flowers.

"So if she failed this class once, why would she take it again?" I asked, as I perched on one of the benches. Beads of rainwater from the night before still dotted the seat, so I didn't slide back far. "I mean, she must not have liked the class, so why put herself through it again."

Alice leaned against the brick wall of the building and tilted her face up to the sun. "We don't just take classes we like. To graduate, you have to take classes in a lot of different areas. I think Ashley's majoring in kinesiology."

"Wh—?"

"It's like gym for grown-ups. For people who want to be personal trainers or work for sports teams." I thought that sounded like a pretty cool job, actually, and probably pretty lucrative, but Alice described it with complete disdain. "But everyone has to take a literature class to graduate, even the gym rats."

I glanced down at my watch. "Wow. Our reprieve is almost up. Back to the salt mines, kiddo."

She sighed. "I thought this would be a great summer."

I wrapped my arm around her neck in a playful headlock, careful not to spill soda on her twinset or her shiny hair. "It is a great summer. You've got the coolest job ever. And this teaching assistant thing is not too shabby, either."

"Ha, ha."

I planted a kiss on the side of her head. "Don't let this Reggie character get you down, Alice," I whispered against her hair.

She pulled away and yanked open the door for me. "Just another fish in the sea?" she asked.

"Not even that. Just another bubble in a sea of fish farts."

That drew a genuine laugh from her lips. "I'm not sure all men are fish farts," she said. "But we sure know how to pick 'em."

"Amen."

Twenty

Finn called me late that afternoon. His voice held equal parts fatigue and excitement.

"I found something on Ostergard's blog," he announced without preamble. "I don't know if it's motive for murder, but it'll make one hell of a feature story for the *News-Letter*."

We arranged to meet back at Sinclair Hall to confront Landry together. I called ahead to arrange the meeting, using the fund-raiser for Bryan as a pretext.

Landry greeted us in the hallway outside the English Department office. He offered me a tight smile, but didn't offer his hand to either of us.

"Mr. Harper, isn't it? I wasn't expecting you. Are you doing a story on the benefit?"

"I'm afraid not, Dr. Landry," Finn said. "Maybe we should discuss this in private?"

Landry glanced over our shoulders toward the door, as though he were contemplating making a run for it, but ultimately he pasted a wan smile on his face and led us through the maze of hallways to his office.

Given his stature in the department, he commanded a corner office, complete with a brass nameplate on the wall.

Inside, the decor reflected his interest in Scandinavian film. Austere black and white landscapes covered the walls and a large, bare glass-topped desk dominated the space.

Landry gestured for us to take the slim wooden side chairs set before the desk, while he settled into the black leather seat behind it.

"Dr. Landry," Finn said, "I'm gonna cut to the chase here. We know that you fabricated the interviews in your book."

"Excuse me?"

Landry might study film, but he lacked acting skills. His effort at outrage fell completely flat, and there wasn't a hint of surprise on his face.

"You thanked Walder Ostergard for arranging your interviews with Rasmussen, but in the months before you allegedly met with Rasmussen, Ostergard was on location in Romania, working on a film for some Spanish director."

Landry waved his hand dismissively. "Mr. Harper, surely in this day and age you don't think a little thing like an ocean would prevent me from communicating with Ostergard."

"Hmmm. And how did you do that? Did you manage to fly to Romania and back some weekend, in between teaching your classes and managing the university's search for a new provost?"

"No, actually. I had no need to travel. The Internet is a wonderful thing."

Finn smiled, a cat with a rat in his grasp. "It is. Walder Ostergard certainly thought so. He blogged almost every day, except for those months he was in Romania."

"Oh?" I detected a faint tremor in Landry's voice.

"Yessiree. Big ol' gap in the blog for those months. Which he explained on his return to LA. He offered a rather colorful account of the mountainous area in which they filmed and its utter lack of modern amenities. Such as Internet connections."

Landry shrugged. "I don't know how regular his access was, but I assure you we managed to connect during his time there. He must have taken a weekend in Bucharest at some point."

"Maybe," Finn conceded. "But the funny thing is that he

mentions talking to you on his blog. It's just six months after you allegedly met with Rasmussen. He ranted about another foolish intellectual, this one from Texas of all places, trying to use him to get to Rasmussen. He didn't have very kind things to say about your parentage, I'm afraid."

The color drained from Landry's face.

"Emily commented once about how long it took you to get that book done and out the door. You'd completed the interviews so long ago, why didn't you just finish the manuscript? But I'm guessing you were waiting for both Rasmussen and Ostergard to die so you could spin your story of getting the interviews without anyone around to refute it. But you didn't count on Ostergard blogging about everything from world politics to his bathroom habits. And you didn't count on his blog staying up and accessible after his death."

At first, Landry didn't respond. The dark eyes behind his spectacles glittered with calculation. He steepled his hands and gently tapped his lips with his forefingers. I must admit I felt a stab of joy watching him squirm. I didn't imagine Sally Landry would thank me, but I felt as though we were defending her honor.

"What do you want?" he said finally.

Finn laughed. "Just the truth."

"Right," Landry scoffed.

I jumped in then. "Bryan figured out what you'd done, didn't he? And that's why you killed him."

"What? Good lord, I didn't kill anyone!"

Finn shrugged. "I think we'll just have to let the police figure that one out."

And I planned to tell the police that Landry had eaten dinner at a swanky Italian restaurant the night Emily died. The night I found a serving of restaurant tiramisu on her kitchen counter. After all, if Landry killed Bryan to cover his fraud, he could have just as easily killed Emily for the same reason.

"No," Landry pleaded. "I didn't kill Bryan. He...He did know that the interviews were faked, but we'd reached an agreement."

"Blackmail?" Finn asked.

"Of a sort," Landry conceded.

I felt a thrill of excitement. I couldn't believe I'd been right that night at the Bar None. I had suspected that Bryan had been blackmailing Landry, I'd just been wrong about the subject of the extortion.

"Bryan knew better than to ask for money," Landry continued. "Teaching isn't especially lucrative. But he needed something more than money. He needed my support in the department. I passed him on his exams, even though his answers were execrable, and I agreed to support him in his appeal of failure."

Finn straightened. "You were going to help him destroy Emily Clowper's career?"

Landry looked pained. "He hardly needed my help. She was the only one who voted to fail him, so even if Gunderson and I tried to remain neutral, our approval of his initial answers alone made her look guilty. I tried to make Emily see the futility of her position, but she was so obstinate."

That solved one mystery. Emily had been the lone holdout, the only person standing between Bryan and his graduate career.

Finn narrowed his eyes. "Blackmailers don't usually settle for one payment. They come back to the well again and again."

"Not Bryan. Look, I told you, I didn't have money to give the boy, and he didn't seem to need it. He seemed pretty flush with cash, actually. And he had an incentive to keep my secret. The success of this book will make my career and put Dickerson's graduate program on the map. Bryan was hitching his wagon to my star. Destroying my career would hurt him, too.

"Besides," he said, "I couldn't have killed Bryan. I was supposed to have brunch that morning with the college's media representative. He didn't show, but from ten until after noon, I was across campus at the faculty club dining room."

"Brunch by yourself. That's not much of an alibi," Finn said. "Do you have a receipt?"

Landry's face fell, but almost as quickly, a grin spread across his face. "No, no receipt. But I used my i-Cash. There should be a record of my initial order and my dessert order in the university's computer system."

Finn stood, and I followed suit. "Like I said, we'll let the police sort this out."

"I'm begging you," Landry said. "You don't have any reason to care about me, but I know you care about this town and this school. Another scandal will destroy the whole community."

Finn stepped aside to allow me to leave ahead of him, but I stopped in the doorway and stared down Landry. "You're underestimating the strength of this town," I said. "Ain't nothing you can throw at us that will destroy us."

I left then, with Finn hot on my heels.

When we reached the parking lot, I spun around to face Finn

"You're not going to let him skate on this, are you?"

"Oh, hell no," Finn replied. "I'll wait until after the benefit for Bryan, so that Landry can help drum up money and Cal's family can have an evening of peace."

He tipped back his head, and I almost gasped at the rage in Finn's eyes. Rage and pain.

"But after the benefit, I'm gonna nail that jerk to the wall for what he did to Emily."

Twenty-One

I'd never thought of Alice as the swooning type, but when Kyle confidently declared he could hack into the Dickerson i-Cash system, she came darn close.

Finn gave the kid a high-five.

"I'm gonna pretend I didn't hear any of that," I said. "This is supposed to be your wholesome activity, working at the A-la-mode to keep you out of trouble. Your mama would have my hide if she knew I was contributing to your delinquency."

Kyle smirked. "Even if you told my mom what I did, she wouldn't understand."

I felt a pang of sympathy for his mom. I didn't understand one hundred percent what he planned to do, but I knew it couldn't possibly be legal.

"I'm going to need a faster connection than McKlesky and Howard's crappy open Wi-Fi network. We've got good service at home."

"I'm coming with you," Alice said.

"Nuh-uh. You're not going anywhere," Bree said. "At least, not without me."

Kyle looked nervously between Bree and Alice. He'd witnessed their verbal brawls before, and I could tell he didn't much fancy being caught in the middle of one.

To everyone's relief, Alice didn't put up a fuss. "Oh, all right. You can come, too."

"Hey," I said. "You can't all leave me here on my own."

It was a Wednesday night, unlikely to be particularly busy, but we had a rule that no one worked the store alone after dark. Even me.

"I can help," Finn offered.

Bree laughed. "Help yourself to a vat of ice cream, most likely." We'd all made a conscious effort to tease Finn, to keep him from dwelling too much on the loss of his friend.

Finn drew himself up in mock indignation. "I beg your pardon. I can roll up my sleeves and dip cones with the best of 'em."

"Mmmm-hmmm," she drawled. "Something tells me you've never done a lick of manual labor in your life."

He clasped his hands over his heart and staggered back. "You wound me, Bree." He opened one loden green eye. "Though you are absolutely correct." He laughed and stood up. "There's a first time for everything, right Tally?"

"I guess we're gonna find out," I said.

Finn worked hard that night. I hadn't counted on a rush of families following the curtain coming down on the community theater's production of Alice in Wonderland. Wound-up kids and their harried parents swarmed the store, and both Finn and I were up to our armpits in junior sundaes for over an hour.

As the worst of the kid frenzy died down, I sent Finn to the back of the store to take a breather. The minute he disappeared, Rosemary and George Gunderson arrived with another couple. The two ladies tumbled through the door, arm in arm, their heads tipped together in eager conversation, while the men hung back and played the courtly gentlemen.

In their evening finery, the foursome stood out in the sea of golf shirts and jeans: Dr. Gunderson sported a natty tweed jacket and a bow tie, and Mrs. Gunderson wore a beaded satin shell and long velvet skirt, both in a refined wine color. Beauty parlor curls gave volume to her wintry white hair, and pearls the size of garbanzo beans studded her ears. She carried a small gold cake box in one hand and a beaded clutch in the other.

The other couple was also decked out in fancy clothes. He in a brass-buttoned navy blazer and Kelly green and navy striped tie, she in a peacock blue chiffon-skirted cocktail dress and a towering hairdo of golden blonde curls—but they blended a little better. It's hard to put my finger on the differences, but the Gundersons just didn't look like they belonged in Dalliance, Texas. Too much polish, not enough sparkle.

I greeted them with a big smile, and received one from Rosemary in return. George wore his usual dour expression, but I was learning not to take it personally.

"Tallulah Jones," Rosemary said. "We've come to celebrate!"

"I can see that," I said with a chuckle. The flush on the ladies' cheeks and the twinkle in their eyes suggested at least one bottle of champagne for the evening.

Rosemary leaned across the counter conspiratorially. "The Grants, Hazel and Jim, have been married for forty years," she said in a stage whisper.

"Hush, Rosie," Hazel said. "You'll have everyone doing the math and figuring out what an old lady I am."

Rosemary giggled. "Nonsense. You were a child bride, after all."

The two women laughed delightedly, while Jim and George Gunderson looked on with small smiles of indulgence.

"I'm so glad you decided to celebrate your fortieth with us," I said.

Hazel stepped back and rested a hand on her husband's arm. "On our very first date, Jim took me to an ice cream parlor after our movie. One malt, two straws."

The soft smile on her face as she looked into Jim's eyes

made me melt a little. That one tiny twist of her lips spoke volumes of moonlit walks and gentle teasing and all the thousands of moments of quiet joy that made up a long, happy marriage.

"When Rosie suggested we come here for dessert, the soufflé and tiramisu at the Hickory Tavern lost all their luster."

"I've just heard so many wonderful things," Rosemary explained, "I finally decided I had to try your delicious ice cream myself. And now that you'll be providing dessert for the benefit for Bryan Campbell, George here is intrigued, too."

"The benefit will be an important event for Dickerson," George intoned.

"Yes, I've hardly seen George these past two weeks. He's been working late at the university every night, just like he did before he got tenure."

George's brow wrinkled, but Rosemary gave his arm a little squeeze. "Don't worry, dear. I know your work is important, and Madeline's been keeping me company."

She held up her gold cardboard box. "I hope you don't mind. We decided halfway through dinner that we should come here, but I'd already ordered my lemon soufflé, and I couldn't let it go to waste."

"Oh, of course I don't mind," I said. "What can I get for you?"

"What would you recommend?"

"Well, we make our ice cream using a traditional French pot method, so there's very little air. As a result, it has a dense, velvety texture. It doesn't really need dressing up. A dish of one or two of our signature flavors would be a good choice. My personal favorites are the raspberry mascarpone, the balsamic strawberry, and the dark chocolate/hazelnut. We also serve sundaes—sauced with brandied cherries, salted caramel, or bittersweet fudge, and topped with fresh whipped cream—

milkshakes, and traditional malts."

"Oh, my."

A satisfying response. I smiled.

"What do you think, George?"

He removed his glasses and rested the temple piece against his lip, lowered his lids, and hummed thoughtfully.

I take my ice cream more seriously than most, but even I thought his heavy contemplation went over the top. More like Henry Kissinger considering diplomacy in Southeast Asia than a man considering dessert.

"I suggest," he intoned in a sonorous voice, "we try the raspberry and the chocolate, a scoop of each."

"Excellent choice," I said, smiling right through the urge to roll my eyes.

Hazel snuggled up next to Jim. "We'll have a chocolate malt. Two straws."

I laughed. "Why don't y'all take a seat, and I'll have your ice cream ready in a jiff."

While Hazel and Jim's chocolate malt spun on the mixer, I dished up the Gundersons' ice cream in small pressed-glass dishes and garnished them with complimentary vanilla pizzelles, cookies that looked like small, flat waffle cones.

I could have carried the dishes out in my hands, but I opted to use the tray we kept behind the counter. The mention of the Hickory Tavern reminded me that the Gundersons obviously had some cash to throw around. I hated to be a suck-up, but anything I could do to impress them could ultimately be good for business.

By the time I finished serving the foursome, chatting them up a bit and leaving them happily trading spoons of ice cream like a bunch of kids on their first date, Finn had returned from his break.

"They're cute together, aren't they?" he said.

SCOOP TO KILL   159

"Who? The Grants or the Gundersons?"

"Both, I guess, but I was talking about the Gundersons."

I watched George spoon his cherry onto Rosemary's ice cream. She giggled, and I could see the blush on her cheeks from where I stood.

"Adorable. You know them, right?"

"The Gundersons? Not well." Finn and I leaned against the back counter, watching the happy chaos of the families enjoying their sundaes and cones.

"I thought Rosemary was friends with your mom."

"Yes, but just recently. They met in the hospital when Mom had her first stroke. Rosemary was being treated for breast cancer. She still comes to visit Mom every week, like clockwork, but I don't intrude. Oh, and in between her strokes, Mom had them all over for dinner during one of my visits home. But just once."

"All? I thought it was just George and Rosemary."

"And her niece, Madeline Jackson. I think the Gundersons are from Boston, but their niece went to law school at University of Houston. She moved up to Dalliance when Rosemary got sick." Finn grabbed a dishcloth from the tub of bleach water we kept beneath the counter and began wiping down the dipping wells. "She's basically a daughter to the Gundersons, spending time with Rosemary every day. That's how I knew about Kristen Ver Steeg's practice."

I stared at him blankly. "Who?"

"Kristen Ver Steeg. Bryan's lawyer. She and Madeline Jackson are partners."

Of course. Dalliance had grown over the years, sprawling out from the courthouse square in increasingly wide rings of strip malls and McMansion-filled neighborhoods; but it was still, fundamentally, a small town. You couldn't sneeze without someone's cousin saying "God bless." Now, in the space of just a

few weeks, I'd heard about this new law firm three times: they
were the firm Bryan had hired to handle his dispute with
Dickerson, they were the firm where Crystal's fiancé Jason
would be working this summer, and they were connected to the
Gundersons.

Before I could comment on the small orbit of Dalliance
society, my phone rang. Bree.

"Tally, did you know Kyle is a freakin' genius?"

"I did not." I grabbed another bleachy rag and got to work
on the ledges of the display freezer.

"Well, he is. I don't know what kind of weird voodoo he
worked, but he managed to crack into that i-Cash system in
about ten minutes flat."

"Lord-a-mercy." I didn't even want to think about the sorts
of mischief that boy could get into on the Internet. Identity
theft, credit card fraud; it gave me chills.

"Yep. Turns out that Landry fella was telling the truth. He
used his ID card to buy an egg-white omelet and dry rye toast at
ten fifteen a.m. on the morning Bryan was murdered, and then
he bought a double-chocolate lava cake at eleven thirty. Both at
the faculty club, which according to Alice, is a good twenty
minute walk across campus from Sinclair Hall."

"Huh." The bell above the store door rang as another family
filed out. The evening was winding down. As soon as we got the
place cleaned up, I could head home and do my reading for
class.

Oy. Homework.

"But that's not all we found," Bree continued. "On a whim, I
suggested Kyle look at Emily Clowper's card use. Turns out that
she used her ID card to buy a soft drink from the vending
machine in the basement of Sinclair Hall at eleven fifty-six on
the night she died."

I straightened so fast, I knocked my head on the inside of

the display freezer.

"Ow. What?"

Bree chuckled darkly. "You heard me, sister. Emily Clowper went to campus between the A-la-mode and home."

"But she wasn't allowed on campus," I said.

"Well, that didn't stop her. Whatever she was up to, it must have been important if she risked getting caught in her office when it was off-limits. Wanna bet that whatever she did or whoever she saw there got her killed?"

Twenty-Two

Where Emily Clowper's house had been pristine to the point of barrenness, her office looked like raccoons had been living in it.

The room—if I can be so bold as to call it that, since it was about the size of my walk-in freezer—held a battered metal desk and two dented filing cabinets. The middle drawer of one of the cabinets was wedged open, a spray of paper bursting from its depths, and a drift of still more paper littered the floor. Utilitarian shelves mounted on metal L-brackets lined one wall, their lengths packed with stacks of books, manila file folders, and mismatched three-ring binders. A poster from the Stratford Shakespeare Festival hung in a plastic frame on another wall.

And, mysteriously, a stuffed rooster—the sort you find in truck stops and flea markets across Texas, with a Styrofoam body covered in real chicken feathers and a red felt comb—perched on a corner of the desk, staring balefully at intruders.

"I can't believe I let you talk me into this," I said.

Finn wrapped his arm around my shoulder and gave me a brief squeeze. "I can. Let's face it, Tally, you can't resist a little snooping."

"This isn't 'a little snooping.' This is crazy. Last time we committed a B&E, we got caught, remember? But that was just Wayne's place." Finn, Bree, and I had broken into my ex's office the year before, but we'd managed to talk him out of pressing charges. "I don't think the Dickerson security guards will be so forgiving."

"Relax. No one will catch us. It's a Sunday afternoon. The guards are all probably holed up in the student center watching the Rangers game."

Finn made himself at home behind Emily's desk, and I perused her shelves.

"Are you going to be able to get into her computer?" I asked.

"Uh-huh," Finn muttered. "The system requires a log-in, but Emily always used the same password for everything. Bella."

Her childhood dog.

A renewed sense of anger welled up in me, a desire to punish whoever had ended Emily's life so early. Whoever had prevented her from getting the dog she wanted so much.

"Huh."

"What did you find?" I moved around behind Finn so I could see the computer screen.

"It looks like the last file she had open was a spreadsheet. It's titled EmilyGrant."

I leaned in for a better look. "Sure, she was applying for a grant to go out east to work on her book. Remember, Alice brought her a copy of the proposal on her little keychain thingamabob."

"This spreadsheet was modified the night she died," Finn said. "If Alice brought the files to Emily, why would she come in here to work on it. She could have gotten in trouble if she'd been caught on campus. Why risk it for a file she already had?"

He hit a button on the computer and the spreadsheet disappeared. In its place was a window with little labeled images.

"This is the folder EmilyGrant was saved in." He manipulated the cursor so that it sat on one of the images. "Look, here's another spreadsheet file. Grant_Calc_Temp."

He double-clicked on that image, and another grid of numbers popped up. Another click, and the first spreadsheet appeared side by side with the second.

We both scanned the numbers on the sheet. The notations next to them were gibberish to me, but I could tell that both spreadsheets were basically the same. All except for the numbers at the very bottom of the screen, one labeled F&A and the other labeled Total.

"What's F&A?" I asked.

"I'm not sure." Finn highlighted the number next to F&A on the first spreadsheet, the one labeled EmilyGrant. "It's a formula," he said. "See, right here?" He pointed to a bar across the top of the sheet. "C44 * .485."

He bopped the cursor over to the other spreadsheet, the one labeled Grant_Calc_Temp. "This formula is different. C44 * .49."

"I'm lost," I said.

"Yeah, me too."

"But I know someone who might be able to help us."

I called Alice and wheedled Reggie's number from her. And then I called Reggie. Turned out, he was right down the hall, working in his own office.

"I can't believe you guys broke in here," he said, as he slid into the seat Finn had vacated. Reggie seemed to fit in Emily's office, his unkempt ginger curls a near-perfect match for the fake rooster's red felt comb. And he seemed comfortable behind her desk, mousing around her computer desktop like someone familiar with her filing system.

"We didn't exactly break in," Finn said. "The building was unlocked, and Alice gave us the key to Emily's office."

"Semantics," Reggie muttered.

He studied the two spreadsheets silently for a few minutes, then sighed.

"It's just a math error," he said.

"Explain," Finn commanded.

"This is just a spreadsheet for calculating how much money you need for a project. The research office provides this template"—he pointed at the second spreadsheet—"and you fill in the numbers. See, this is what Emily estimated for her airfare, this is for graduate student assistance, this is for computer equipment."

"What's F&A?" I asked.

"Facilities and Administration. When you get a grant from some outside agency, like the federal government or a nonprofit organization, you ask for the money you, the researcher, will need. Then the school tacks on a percentage to cover the school's costs. They have to hold the money, distribute the checks, audit the researcher's books. That's the 'administration' part. The 'facilities' part is to cover overhead for things like electricity and computer maintenance and stuff like that."

"So why are the two numbers different?" Finn asked.

Reggie shrugged. "This one, the one with the higher number, that's the official spreadsheet the university generates. This other one, that looks like Emily created it herself."

"Oh, right!" I said. "Finn, remember when Alice brought Emily the grant documents? She said she couldn't get to the budget spreadsheet because it was on the university drive, so Emily said she was going to have to recreate it from the printout."

Reggie nodded. "Yeah, this first one you showed me, EmilyGrant, is probably the one that Emily created herself. She just used a different percentage, 48.5 instead of 49, for this calculation."

He picked up a blue folder that was on top of the desk clutter, the words "Summer Grant" scrawled across its front in black marker. He flipped open the folder and pulled out a printed spreadsheet.

"See, if she was recreating this spreadsheet, it looks here like the F&A percentage is 48.5. But apparently in the official spreadsheet, the number is rounded up to 49 before the F&A is calculated."

It looked to me like Emily was in the right and whoever had drafted the official spreadsheet had made the error. I had kept the books for Wayne's Weed and Seed before Wayne Jones and I got divorced, so I knew how easy it was to make an error in a big ol' spreadsheet. I guessed that professional number crunchers could make mistakes just like us little guys.

Reggie spun around in Emily's chair to face us. "Like I said, it's just a math error. No big deal. Now can I get back to work?"

"Sure," Finn said.

Reggie didn't budge.

"You have to leave," he said, waving us toward the door.

Finn and I did as we were told, though Finn pocketed the key to Emily's office. Thankfully, Reggie didn't think to ask for it back.

We trudged out to the parking lot, dejected.

"That got us exactly nowhere," Finn complained.

"Not exactly," I said. "At least now we know that she was working on her grant the night she died. She was making plans for the future. Which means she thought she had a future to plan for."

Finn stopped in his tracks and lowered his head.

"She didn't plan to die," he said softly.

"No. She planned to live."

He pulled me close, wrapped me in his arms. "Thank you," he whispered into my hair.

I just hugged him closer.

Twenty-Three

Emily's parents claimed their daughter and returned to Minnesota. Finn asked if they wanted to stay with him, to linger long enough for a memorial service, but they declined. They were eager to whisk their child away from the place that took her life, and I couldn't blame them.

Ultimately, it became clear that Emily Clowper had no ties to Dalliance beyond the Dickerson campus, and the faculty, staff, and students of the university were ready to put the whole sordid situation behind them. No one wanted to dwell on Emily Clowper's death, and that meant no one particularly wanted to remember her life.

Instead of a memorial service, which would have been all the sadder for the lack of attendants, we decided to honor Emily by helping her parents pack up her earthly possessions.

That Thursday morning, ominous clouds roiled on the horizon, boding a powerful early summer storm. By the time Alice and I got out of class and piled into the van, fat raindrops hit the windshield with an almost purposeful smack, not just falling but diving to earth. We drove slowly through the veils of water to Emily's house.

Finn and Bree were already parked in her driveway. I could just barely make out their shadows in the front seat of Finn's Jeep. When my headlights sliced the gloom, their forms stirred and soon we were all darting through the torrential downpour to the shelter of Emily's wide front porch.

Finn led the way into Emily's living room. I shuddered as the visceral memory of the night of her death welled up inside me. The strange silver-green light of the stormy afternoon cast few shadows in the near-empty room. It felt otherworldly, a mournful dreamscape.

Alice wandered over to a cardboard box next to the faded velvet sofa. She sank down to sit on the bare wood floor tailor-style, her thin pale legs folded beneath her so that I could see the faded scars on her knees, the familiar traces of her childish mishaps. She wore a hint of color on her lips and mascara darkened her golden lashes, but she sprawled on the floor with the artless inelegance of a child.

Without a word, she pulled the box closer, pulled the flaps on top open, and began lifting out books and binders.

"Her parents asked us to send anything that looked personal. Jewelry, photos, scrapbooks. And they said that Emily had a set of china that belonged to her grandmother. They'd like to pass that on to her sister. Everything else, we can donate."

Bree pulled a box of trash bags out of her mammoth purse, pulled a handful of them out of the slit across the top, and set the box on the floor by the front door. "I'll start in the bathroom," she said. "Most of that will be stuff to pitch or donate."

Alice nodded absently, still not saying a word. She kept her head down as she thumbed through a large book that might be a photo album. I didn't see any tears, but something about the brittle set of her shoulders made me think she wept.

Finn bent down and retrieved a couple of trash bags, handed them to me, and picked up a stack of flattened packing boxes. "Bedroom or kitchen?"

A wave of dizziness hit me hard at the very thought of going back into Emily's bedroom. "Kitchen."

He followed me through an empty room that might have held a dining table and into the kitchen. I noticed more this time. The white-painted cabinets with their whimsical handles shaped like eating utensils, the black-and-white checkered vinyl floor, the frilly lavender curtains on the window over the enamel sink. There was something so playful and girly about Emily's kitchen, I wondered if she'd inherited this decor. It seemed inconsistent with her brusque attitude, sharply angled hair, and androgynous eyeglasses.

But then I thought of her flowing dresses and the petal pink of her bicycle, and I could imagine her choosing these items carefully, tiny acts of feminine defiance committed by a woman who refused to fit into a mold.

Finn pulled open a kitchen cupboard and revealed a few boxes of cereal, some canned beans, and a handful of spice jars.

"This isn't going to take long," he said sadly.

I walked past him, pausing to give his shoulder a reassuring squeeze, and opened a pantry filled with instant soup containers and unopened rolls of paper towels.

"She struck me as someone who didn't place much stock in material possessions," I said.

Finn laughed. "You've always been a master of understatement, Tally."

We worked quietly for a bit, throwing away opened packages of food and perishables, boxing up unopened cans and packets for the local food bank, sifting through kitchen gadgets and utensils for those that were worth donating and those that weren't.

Then, out of the clear blue sky, Finn said, "Tell me about this place Peachy's staying."

I paused in the act of stacking a set of plastic measuring cups together, wondering what prompted that question. "It's nice," I said, tucking the neatly nested stack into a box for the local thrift store. "Peachy's in a wing for active seniors. They all have their own apartments with sitting rooms and kitchenettes and separate bedrooms. She can fix her own dinner if she wants, or go down to the dining room. They have game nights and field trips to the movies, and Peachy already has a regular euchre game in her room."

"So she likes it?"

I chuckled. "As much as Peachy likes anything. You know how she is. She's not happy unless she's raising Cain about something or another."

Grandma Peachy had a sweet name but a salty disposition. She swore like a sailor, smoked a pipe, and could shoot straighter than the most grizzled cowboy. She'd had to manage a good-sized ranch and raise a couple of hell-raising daughters all on her own after my Grandpa Clem got sent to the federal pen. It took grit, which Peachy had in spades.

"What about people who can't cook for themselves?" Finn asked.

I shrugged. "That's one of the reasons we wanted Peachy to move into this place now. They have more involved care for people who have physical problems or even dementia. She's healthy as a stoat right now, but if something changes she'll be able to stay put. It was hard enough moving her out of the farmhouse. We're not moving her again until we haul her cranky butt out to the cemetery."

Finn didn't respond. He pulled open the doors of a mint-green painted breakfront. Emily's floral china was stacked neatly inside. I could see the film of dust on them from where I stood.

He silently constructed a cardboard box and secured the bottom with packing tape. He grabbed a roll of paper towels, tossing another one to me. We began pulling dishes out of the cupboard, wrapping them in towels, and tucking them into the box.

"I'm thinking of leaving Dalliance."

He said it so quietly, so matter-of-factly, that his meaning didn't register at first.

I froze, my hands wrapped around a delicate tea cup.

"What?"

"I'm thinking of leaving town. Moving on."

"What about your mom?"

"This was supposed to be a temporary arrangement, just until she got back on her feet. My mom had another checkup with her neurologist. It's been over a year since her last stroke, and she's not getting any better. She's not going to get any better."

He blew out a frustrated breath, pulled the last few dishes out of the box and started to repack them more securely. I watched his big hands manipulate the feminine saucers and bowls. It seemed so intimate, him pulling Emily's treasures from their hiding spot.

"I can't take care of Mom on my own. The home health care workers are great, but there's no continuity there. It's a different woman almost every day. Mom should have people who know her situation taking care of her, people who will notice subtle changes from day to day."

I forced myself to move, to continue packing Emily's dishes.

"Where would you go? Back to Minneapolis?"

"No. There's nothing waiting for me there. Maybe Chicago or Atlanta."

"I see."

"Dammit Tally, don't take that tone with me."

"What tone?" I asked, genuinely confused. The thought of Finn leaving town left me bereft. But more than hurt, I had a sense of déjà vu.

With Finn's chin set at a defiant angle and a fire burning

behind his moss-green eyes, his expression transported me through the years to a sultry summer evening during our senior year in high school.

Finn telling me he was going to travel the world instead of staying in Texas for college. Me telling Finn that I couldn't go with him. That it was over. Finn tearing off into the darkness, lost to me until he showed up on my doorstep the autumn after my divorce.

Here we go again, I thought.

"You've got that tone like I've disappointed you," Finn snapped.

I tore a sheaf of paper towels from the roll. "Of course I'm disappointed," I said. "Dalliance is a better place with you in it. But you didn't disappoint me."

He grunted.

"Really. I'm not in a position to have any expectations of you, Finn."

He cut his eyes to the side, studying me.

"Is that so?"

I sighed. "Isn't it? Dang, Finn. You disappeared for seventeen years, and when you pop back up, you act like you never left. Like we can just pick right up and be buddies. But we've changed, both of us. I think I like the man you became, but I don't even really know you anymore."

"Do you want to?"

His question stopped me in my tracks. I knew that my answer mattered. A lot.

I sighed. "Of course I want to know you, Finn. But it'll take time. Are you willing to give it time?"

He stepped away, pulled open the refrigerator and began tossing cartons of yogurt and half-used jars of salad dressing into a garbage bag.

"I don't feel like I have time, Tally."

I could barely hear his words, but the thread of pain in his voice was clear as day.

I set down the half-wrapped plate I held and crossed the few steps to his side.

"Finn, none of us know how much time we have, which is why we need to relish every minute. Maybe you need to get out of this town to be happy. Maybe you need a big city and an exciting job. That's okay. I won't hold you back. I'll miss you, but I would never begrudge you going after your dream."

I hugged him, but he stayed stiff in my arms.

"Just promise me you won't make a decision about your future while you're in the midst of this grief. Let yourself mourn for Emily. Get on your feet before you take a step."

For a second, he sagged in my grasp. Then he cleared his throat of tears.

"I'm going to clean out her bedroom," he said. "Can you finish in here?"

I was torn between relief that he didn't want me to accompany him into the room where she died and hurt that he didn't need me by his side.

"Sure, Finn. You go ahead. I'll be right here."

As he walked away, I wondered if he'd come back. And I wondered how long I could wait.

Twenty-Four

Thanks to the condensed schedule of the May-term class, we had our final exam a mere three weeks after we started class, on the last day of May. I'd been trying to keep up with the work. Alice wouldn't grade my test, of course, but she'd see my grades, and I didn't want to look like an idiot.

Cal and I had all the plans for Bryan's benefit sewn up, and after our strikeout in Emily's office, Finn had left me alone about Bryan and Emily's murders. But between class time and keeping the A-la-mode afloat, I was in the weeds. When Ashley asked me if I wanted to study with her, I jumped on the chance.

She stopped by the store at ten, as we were closing up. I sent Bree and Kyle on home, so we'd have quiet, and we settled into a booth in the dining room.

Ashley pulled a couple of cans out of her bag, tall beverage cans, black with orange flames licking up the sides and acid-green lettering. "For energy," she said, pushing one toward me. "Can't study without it."

Curious, I read the label. The can promised me lasting energy with no crash, but caffeine and sugar were pretty high on the list of ingredients.

I cracked open the can and took a sip. It tasted like pure evil. I let the liquid dribble back into the can rather than swallow it. That sort of crap might be fine for young people, but my stomach couldn't handle it. I'd stick to good ol' diet soda.

I didn't want to be rude, though, so for the first couple of hours of our study session, I'd occasionally lift the can to my lips and pretend to take a drink. Finally, though, I needed some caffeine for real, so I offered to get us sodas.

Ashley tipped her head back to drain the last dregs of her energy drink. "That would be great."

While I got our drinks, I made small talk. "Your folks must be really proud of you, almost ready to graduate."

"Hunh," she grunted noncommittally. "They'd be a lot prouder if I'd graduated on time."

I didn't challenge her, but she went on as though I had. "I know I'm not the smartest person in the world," Ashley said. "I didn't even want to go to college. But you can't get a good job without a degree anymore."

I guessed that depended on your definition of a "good job." My friend Angel didn't have a college degree and she'd just started a new job at Erma's Fry by Night Diner, but I imagined "short order cook" would not make the cut in Ashley's world.

"I had it all figured out," she continued.

"Yeah? What are planning to do when you graduate?" I handed a can of diet soda to Ashley and popped open my own.

"When we were freshmen, we had to take all these personality tests to find our strengths and figure out what we were passionate about." Ashley took a sip of her drink. "I'm good at motivating other people and organization, and I really love health and fitness. So I decided I wanted to work in the fitness industry."

"And that's why you got that job at the Lady Shapers?"

"Right. I started off working at the desk and doing personal training, but I did an unpaid internship last summer in their corporate office. And I'm double-majoring in kinesiology and marketing." She set down the can, picked up her pen, and started doodling on the open page of her notebook. "I've been working hard, trying to get good grades, and doing all the networking stuff we're supposed to do so we know the right people."

I had to hand it to her. Ashley Henderson might not be destined for a Nobel Prize, but she seemed to have a grip on what she wanted to do with her life and how to go about getting it. When I was her age, I wasn't nearly so focused.

Heck, I still wasn't.

"So do you have a job lined up for after graduation? I know it's a tough market out there."

Her lower lip quivered, but then she took a deep breath, narrowing her eyes as she exhaled. Misery or anger, and she chose anger.

"I did have a job," she said. "A spot opened up in the management trainee program at FitFab. But not anymore." A muscle in her jaw twitched.

"Oh, dear. What happened?"

"This stupid class happened," she spat. "Stupid, stupid, stupid." She punctuated each "stupid" by stabbing her notebook with her pen.

"I have to take this dumb class for my degree. Who even cares about this stuff? A bunch of boring books written by guys who are dead. If I really wanted to know this story"—she picked up her copy of The Age of Innocence and waved it around—"I would watch the movie, right? I looked it up. It has that lady from that Johnny Depp movie in it."

I had no idea what she was talking about, but I nodded along. The girl had lost a job, and she was plenty pissed.

"This class is an intro class. Intro! But that…that…man wanted us to know all sorts of stuff about these books. Like about symbols and shit. I just couldn't do what he wanted and do well in my real classes and do well at the Lady Shapers."

I assumed "that man" was Bryan Campbell. Alice had said

Ashley took the class from Bryan during the fall semester, and both Alice and Emily said he had unreasonable expectations of his students.

"Sure," I said soothingly. "You're only one girl."

That took some of the starch out of her sails, and her lip pooched out in a childish pout.

"Exactly. I asked him for help, and he said I could have an incomplete. I thought, 'Great, I'll write an extra couple of papers and then he'll give me my C minus, and it will be okay.'"

Her emotions were rocketing all over the place, making me extra glad I hadn't consumed that so-called energy drink. Now, tears welled up in her eyes. She was close enough to Alice's age that I had to fight the urge to wrap my arms around her and mother her.

"I worked all term on those papers, three of them! And he still said my class average was a 69.49. Can you believe it? Just a smidge higher, 69.5, and he would have rounded up to 70 and I would have passed. But instead, I got a D plus."

"That's not passing? I thought anything more than an 'F' was passing."

"Not for requirements. You have to get a C minus or higher for it to count. Stupid!" Her pen attacked her notebook with sudden ferocity. "I begged him—begged him!—to give me the C minus. I was so close!"

I nodded again and made a soothing sound in the back of my throat.

"But he said no. I told him it was, what's the word, arbitrary? to say that a 69.49 was failing and a 69.5 was passing, but he said that everything was arbitrary." She scrunched up her face and spoke in a mocking, whining voice that was clearly supposed to be Bryan's. "Why do your shoes cost eighty dollars instead of seventy-nine ninety-nine? Why does the bank give you 2.99 percent interest instead of 3 percent? It's just a fraction of a percent on paper, but that tiny fraction can represent a real difference." She shook her head and slipped back into her own voice. "Maybe it's a real difference when it's money, but this wasn't money. Just points, and those aren't real things."

I could see both sides, and I sensed a philosophical dimension that I didn't particularly want to tackle at half past midnight on a school night.

"So FitFab retracted your job offer?"

A tear slipped from one mascaraed eye and made a sooty track down her cheek. "Yes. The training program is only offered every six months, at the corporate office in Chattanooga. I was supposed to start next Monday, but instead I'll still be in school."

"Can you do the program in the fall?"

She shrugged her shoulders and sniffed. "No, this was it. My only shot. And now it's gone."

I'd spent enough time around Alice to know that teenage girls have a very black-or-white view of the world. That one pair of size six jeans fits a little snug? You must be super fat and completely gross. The cute boy doesn't ask you to dance? You must be hideous and totally unlovable.

Ashley wasn't strictly a teenager, but close enough.

I also knew that anything I might say, any logical argument I might make, would prompt a storm of tears and rage about how I just didn't understand. So I kept my lips shut.

"My life is over," Ashley concluded.

The tears were coming faster now, and she suddenly went white as a ghost. "Oh, God," she muttered, then pushed away from the table and dashed for the bathroom.

I briefly considered following her, weighing her need for comfort and her need for dignity. On the one hand, I was her peer in class, not her mama. On the other hand, her mama wasn't here, and I was.

Ultimately, my desire not to completely embarrass myself on the midterm exam won out. I spent the next ten minutes reading through my notes and skimming over the passages I had dog-eared in my books, until Ashley returned. Her face was still pasty white, but she'd dried her tears and seemed to be together.

"You want something to eat?" I might not want to hug the girl, but at least I could feed her. "We've got ice cream, of course. And crackers and fruit in the back."

Her face creased in a pained expression. "Maybe some crackers?"

I gave her a teasing wink. "Sure I can't convince you to try a little ice cream? Lots of calcium," I prodded.

"No, thanks. I'm getting really fat. Completely gross."

Before I could restrain myself, a laugh escaped me. It was, of course, the wrong thing to do. Her face clouded over, and I rushed to smooth her ruffled feathers.

"Oh, honey, you are so far from fat. Trust me."

She looked uncertain, like she desperately wanted to believe me but just couldn't bring herself to do it.

Before we could wander down the rabbit trail of adolescent female body image, I hustled to the back of the store and grabbed the stash of crackers.

"Now," I said, plopping the box down on the table between our books, "can you explain the effect of the first World War on the Harlem Renaissance? Because I sure can't."

Twenty-Five

Generally speaking, the May-term American Lit students weren't Dickerson's A-team. But apparently we all had strong motivation to pass that exam, because when I arrived at Sinclair Hall the morning of the test, the overwhelming majority of my classmates were already in their seats, ready to rock. They all bent over their notebooks, looks of pained concentration plastered on their faces, cramming frantically.

All, that is, except for Ashley Henderson.

Ashley rested her forehead on her desk as though she felt ill. Her hair was greasy, her skin blotchy, her clothes even more disheveled than ever.

It was so quiet in that room, you could hear a rat piss on cotton. Until Bubba arrived. He slid into the seat behind Ashley and gave her chair a nudge with his foot.

"Hey, Ash, you all set for the test," he drawled.

She didn't move except to raise one hand in the one-fingered salute.

He laughed, and elbowed his buddy in the next seat. "Ashley doesn't have to worry. She can earn an 'A' with extra credit." They all cackled like this was some sort of hilarious joke.

"Shut. Up."

I took the seat right next to her. "Are you okay?" I asked.

She moaned.

Reggie pushed through the door at the back of the

classroom, Alice trailing in his wake. "Good morning, students. Are we all set?"

A collective groan filled the room, but beneath that sound I caught a whimper from Ashley. "Oh, God," she muttered before she fumbled her way out of her seat, clawed her way over my legs, and dashed up the stairs, shoving both Reggie and Alice out of her way as she went.

The whole class watched her push through the door and disappear. When the door squealed on its hinges as it swung shut, a few students chuckled nervously. Then, from the hall, we all heard the unmistakable sound of retching. The chuckles turned into groans of disgust.

Reggie appeared flummoxed. He looked at Alice, who shook her head tightly. Apparently she did not consider playing nursemaid to Ashley part of her job description.

They both looked at me.

I sighed.

Sure, from the university's perspective, I was just another undergrad. But I was the oldest person in the room, and even though I didn't have children of my own, my very presence screamed "mom." Who better to follow poor Ashley?

Besides, I thought, maybe if I helped Reggie out here, he'd cut me some slack when he graded my exam.

The hallway was empty, but I made an educated guess and headed toward the ladies' room at the end of the hall.

No Ashley.

I stepped back into the hallway and got my bearings. If I were a vomiting coed, where would I go?

As I scanned the hall, I noticed the unisex bathroom at the far end of the hall, down past the English Department main office.

I jogged down the hall and knocked softly on the door. From inside, I heard the sound of more retching.

"Ashley? Honey, it's Tally. Can I get you something?"

"Go away."

"Oh, sweetie, I'm not gonna leave you like this. Do you need a doctor? Can I call your mama for you?"

"No!" The lock clicked, the door opened, and Ashley stuck her face out. Her skin was the color of an unripe honeydew, and her ponytail had fallen out, tangles of dirty blonde hair trailing over her shoulders. "I'll be fine in a few minutes. Just leave me alone, okay?"

I shuffled my feet. I was pretty sure Ashley needed help, and I'd been sent on a mission to rescue her. But she didn't want rescuing. I didn't know what to do.

"Are you sure?"

"I'm," her hand flew to her hair as she spun around and took a few faltering steps toward the toilet. "Oh, God," she moaned as she sank to her knees.

I slipped through the still-open door, closed and locked it behind me, and then held her hair back as she hugged the bowl and heaved.

When the worst of the spasms subsided, I pulled a wad of paper towels from the dispenser, soaked them in cool water from the tap, and pressed them to the back of her neck.

"How far along are you?" I asked.

She stiffened, as though she might deny it, but then collapsed in sobs.

"Five months," she wailed.

I felt every day of my thirty-eight years as I crouched down on that tile floor, pulled Ashley Henderson into my arms, and let her cry it out.

"Does your mama know?" I asked softly.

"No," she whispered. "I didn't know until a couple of weeks ago. Lots of the girls miss their periods when they're working out a lot, and I was training hard so I'd look good for the training program with FitFab. I haven't even seen my mom since I found out. And I, I just can't tell her."

"I understand."

I did. I had never been in Ashley's shoes, but I had been Bree's confidante during her high school pregnancy scare. I could still remember how that tiny little plastic stick brought my bold-as-brass cousin to her knees.

"My life is over," she whimpered.

"Oh, no, honey. It's not."

Of course, the life she had planned for with her carefully chosen majors and her patient networking, the life where she jumpstarted her career in the fitness industry by heading off to Chattanooga without a backward glance; that life was over. But another life, maybe with a baby and definitely with a lot more perspective, had just started.

I didn't bother to point that out, though. At that moment, she needed to mourn the future she'd been planning for.

"It is," she insisted. "I missed the FitFab training program, and when the next one happens, I'll have a little baby. I won't be able to go." Her voice rose steadily as she spoke and her body grew stiff in my grasp. "I'll be stuck here forever."

"Shhh," I soothed. "You'll make yourself sick."

The tension seeped from her. "What am I going to do?" she asked softly.

It wasn't my place to advise this child. She wasn't mine. I barely knew her.

"First thing we're going to do is get you some help. I know you're scared to tell your mother, but trust me, she'll want to know. And she'll love you all the way through this."

She nodded against my shoulder, and I smiled.

"And what about the daddy? He enjoyed the meal, he ought to pay the check."

Ashley's sobs returned in full force. "He's gone," she cried.

"Gone?" A half dozen possibilities blew through my mind: my granddad disappearing into the prison system, my own daddy leaving us for his other family in Tulsa, Bree's favorite step-daddy leaving on military deployment and never coming back, Alice's daddy running off with an exotic dancer named Spumanti...experience had given the women of the Decker family powerful imaginations when it came to men taking a powder.

Still, Ashley took me by surprise when she choked the word "dead" through her tears.

"Dead?" I repeated. She nodded.

Was it...? No. Couldn't be.

But then I remembered the blonde ponytail on the mourner at Bryan's funeral, the one who broke into hysterics at the mention of the grandchildren Bryan's mother would never have.

"Ashley, honey, was Bryan Campbell the father?"

The intensity of her weeping gave me my answer, but she confirmed it by nodding again. Then she pulled out of my embrace and wrapped her fingers around my forearms, tight. Her eyes were wild with panic, the whites showing all the way around the irises.

"Oh, God," she gasped. "You can't tell anyone. Promise me!"

Just the year before I'd witnessed the heartache and havoc caused by keeping secrets about babies. I couldn't promise to keep Ashley's secret. Poor Marla and Steve would be crushed to learn that their son had slept with a student and gotten her pregnant, but the promise of grandchild would go a long way to softening the blow.

"You have to promise me you won't tell his parents," she insisted. "Even Bryan wasn't going to tell them, because they'd insist on keeping the baby. And I, I don't know what I want, but I, I don't want them to know."

She was tripping over her words, but I knew what she meant. And she was right. Steve and Marla—check that, Marla—would insist on being a part of this child's life. If Ashley wanted to give the child up for adoption, Marla would try to get custody and the child would grow up surrounded by a whole community of people who knew the circumstances of his birth. Or if Ashley wanted to keep the baby, she'd be tied to Marla and Steve, people she didn't even know, for the rest of her life.

Wait.

"Ashley, did you tell Bryan you were pregnant?"

She gave me a "get real" look. "Of course I told him," she said. "The minute I found out. I thought maybe he'd feel bad and change my grade for me. But he wouldn't."

Wow. I couldn't tell whether that was a sign that Bryan had principles or a sign that he was a coldhearted jerk. Or both.

"He said it was too late," she continued. "If he turned in a change-of-grade form, he'd have to provide a reason and get it past a bunch of administrators."

I didn't buy that. Oh, I believed Bryan fed her that line, but I didn't believe it was actually true. I had a sneaking suspicion Bryan could have changed her grade if he wanted to. He could have chalked it up to a math error, for crying out loud. But he wouldn't want to give up that tiny bit of power he had over Ashley, wouldn't want her to "win."

"You could have reported him to the department chair," I said.

She rolled her eyes. "Duh. But Bryan said, 'How do I even know that baby is mine? I don't even know you're pregnant.' And I said I can do a DNA test. And he said, 'Not until the baby's born.'"

Bryan raised a good point, God rest his soul.

"Are you sure the baby is Bryan's?"

"Yes," she huffed. "I hooked up with him at the Bar None

just before Christmas. I called him Dr. Campbell and everything, because I knew he got a kick out of being the big professor."

Aha. So Ashley was the girl Bryan had hooked up with the night he went out with the debating crowd. Crystal had seen them, and she knew who Ashley was. No wonder Crystal had been so certain that the girl Bryan left with wasn't a girlfriend.

"I figured it wouldn't hurt," Ashley continued. "I'd stroke his ego a bit, have a little fun with him. He was kind of cute, and it was fun breaking the rules like that. And I thought maybe he'd even give me a pass on the extra papers." She snorted. "Of course he didn't. When I saw him at the start of spring semester in January, he acted like it never even happened."

She pulled a dozen sheets of toilet tissue off the roll, mopped her eyes, and blew her nose. "During the first part of the semester, I was busy with my FitFab application and all the interviews, so I wasn't going out to the bar. And then I started feeling sick so much that I didn't go out. It never occurred to me that I was..." She trailed off and bit her lip, like she didn't want to let the word escape her mouth.

"Pregnant?" I offered.

"Yeah. It had been months since Bryan and I hooked up, and I hadn't been with anyone else. I thought you got sick during the first three months."

I pulled a face. "Everyone's different," I said.

"Apparently. Anyway, Bryan is the only guy I've slept with since, like, last August. And I haven't been this way since August." She pulled her sweatshirt down tight against her body so I could see her tiny baby bump.

Poor Ashley. Bryan got her pregnant and then refused to do the one thing that could make her situation right, give her the grade that would salvage her job with FitFab.

If I had been in Ashley's sneakers, I would have been angry.

Beyond angry.

Livid.

I thought of Ashley stabbing her notebook with her pen as she ranted about the injustice of having to pass American Lit in order to keep her job. With all those pregnancy hormones coursing through her veins and a body made strong by hours at the gym, she could have easily killed Bryan in a fit of rage.

"Did you tell the police about your situation?" I asked carefully.

"What? Why would I?" Her eyes went wide again as she got my drift. "Oh, God! You don't think I killed him, do you? I mean, I absolutely did not kill him." She underscored every word with a vehement shake of her head.

I held up a placating hand, not wanting her to get all riled up again. "You had every right to be angry."

"Duh," she said. I was starting to wonder whether the Dickerson faculty taught that particular rhetorical argument in the classroom.

"Bryan should have done the right thing," I said.

"The right thing? What's that?" she scoffed. "Look, I may not be a genius, but I'm not stupid. Believe me, I thought about getting revenge on Bryan." She held up a hand. "Not by killing him, but by ruining him."

She'd seemed so surprised by the very notion that I might suspect her of murder that I tended to believe Ashley was innocent. Of course, my gut had steered me wrong before, and I was already figuring out when and how to tell Cal about Ashley's relationship with Bryan. But, again, Ashley didn't need to know that right at the moment.

"If you were worried about people believing he was the father, how could you ruin him?"

She shook her head pityingly. "First off, on the Internet, you don't need any proof. I could have told the whole world Bryan Campbell liked to diddle wild coyotes, posted it on

Dickerson D-L anonymously, and I wouldn't need a lick of evidence."

"Dickerson D-L?"

"The Dickerson Down-Low. It's a gossip site for the students here. You can post anonymously and say whatever you want."

Charming.

"Besides," she continued, "even if I didn't have proof the baby was his, I could have reported him to the administration. I'm sure someone saw us at the Bar None. It would have been enough to ruin his credibility and scuttle his own sexual harassment charge against Dr. Clowper."

I hadn't even considered the irony of Bryan taking advantage of his own student while he brought a false claim against Emily Clowper for the very same thing. That took balls. Big brass ones.

"If I'd told on Bryan," Ashley said, "I still probably wouldn't have graduated. At least, not in time for me to get to Chattanooga. If I kept quiet and kept him on my good side, he could actually help me."

"Financially?"

"Yeah. He said he wasn't ready to be a dad, but if the baby was his, he'd take care of us."

Us. She rested her hand on her tummy, the first sign of maternal instinct I'd seen from her. She might not be ready to name her situation, to say the "p" word out loud, but on some level she'd come to grips with the fact that another little person depended on her now.

She turned away from me to study herself in the bathroom mirror. She pushed her hair out of her face and stuck her tongue out at her own reflection. It was a childlike thing to do, and it made my heart crack with pain for her.

With a sigh, she cranked the handle for the hot water and

held one hand beneath the flow while she waited for the warm to work its way to the tap.

"I gave him a hard time about needing to get a real job, but he insisted he had money coming. Real money. The sort of money that would mean I didn't have to worry about that job with FitFab."

I couldn't imagine that Bryan would get much from the university for his complaint against Emily Clowper, especially if the university was on the verge of passing him on his exams. If he got what he wanted in the first place—to move forward in the graduate program—he wouldn't have much in the way of an injury that required financial compensation. And Jonas Landry had sworn Bryan hadn't been blackmailing him for cash. Maybe Bryan had another, more lucrative iron in the fire.

"Did he say where that money was coming from?"

Ashley splashed water on her face, but the streaks of mascara didn't fade a bit. "Nope," she said. "And now I'll never know."

Twenty-Six

Cal handled the news of Ashley's pregnancy better than I would have thought.

By which I mean that he didn't actually, literally bite my head off.

"Dammit, Tally, how the holy hell do you end up in the middle of every goddam mess in this whole goddam town?"

"Settle down, cowboy. I'm not in the middle of anything here." We were sitting at a table near the front of Erma's Fry by Night, digging in to matching Denver omelets, and I didn't cotton much to all the old-timers at the lunch counter listening to Cal dress me down.

"Maybe we gotta break out that dictionary again? Look up 'middle'? Because the way I see it this Ashley girl has a secret that needs telling, and you're the one whose lips are moving."

"Believe me, Cal, I don't particularly want to be sitting here having this conversation. But through no fault of my own, I happen to know she's pregnant. And that she didn't plan to tell your family. Would you have preferred I keep my mouth shut?"

"No," he snapped, dropping his fork to his plate with a bone-jangling crash.

He shoved his fingers through his short salt-and-pepper hair. Men tended to do that a lot when I was around. Not sure why.

He blew out a big breath and picked up his fork again.

"Look, I'm sorry. I'm glad you told me. I just...what was he thinking, Tally?"

I shrugged one shoulder and took a bite of egg. "He's young and male, she's cute and blonde, there might have been alcohol. I doubt thinking had anything to do with it."

"But a student? And he wasn't even safe about it."

I rolled my eyes. "Again, all perfectly good rational arguments which would have meant exactly nothing to that boy in the heat of the moment. Besides, you don't know that he wasn't safe. You can carry an umbrella and still get wet."

Cal choked on a bite of toast, and took a sip of his coffee to wash it down. But by the time he set down his cup, a faint, wistful smile had graced his face.

"Marla will be happy," he said.

"Even under the circumstances?"

"She won't give a rat's ass about the circumstances. All she'll care about is having a grandbaby."

I poked the tines of my fork at my omelet, weighing my words. "I just hope she remembers that Ashley's the mama." Cal narrowed his eyes, bracing for an argument, but I held up a hand to forestall him. "Look, it's between Marla and Ashley. All I'm saying is the girl's as skittish as an unbroke colt, and Marla might get further with her if she slow-played her hand."

He snorted. "I just hope Ashley's feeling skittish and not guilty."

"I really don't think she killed Bryan. And I can't even imagine how or why she would have killed Emily."

"I appreciate your expert opinion, Detective Jones. Since all signs point to Emily Clowper killing Bryan and then taking her own life, I'm inclined to agree with you. But I hope you don't mind if I let the police confirm that story."

"Of course not. Especially since I happen to think Emily Clowper was absolutely innocent and was murdered herself," I said, lifting my coffee cup in a mock salute.

"Good lord, woman. Are you still clinging to that story?"

"It's not a story," I said. "Look, I don't expect you to believe me, but you don't need to make fun of me."

Cal grew serious. "Is that what you think? That I'm making fun of you?"

"Aren't you?"

He shook his head. "No, ma'am. I am not. You follow your own gut. I admire that."

I felt a wave of heat wash up my face. That was quite a compliment coming from Cal, and I didn't know how to respond.

"Now," he said, picking up his fork and pointing it at me, "if you're done playing detective, why don't you tell me about that ice cream cake you're making for tonight."

I laughed, relieved. "Are you gonna pick nits with my cooking now, too?"

He held up his hands in mock surrender. "Darlin', I know when I'm outgunned. I can't boil water without burning it. You cook. I eat."

With everything I had on my plate, I seriously considered letting the American Lit final slide. But I don't like leaving tasks undone, and the thought of failing without trying rankled.

So between brunch with Cal and the fund-raiser for Bryan's scholarship, I found myself back in Sinclair Hall, waiting to take a makeup test.

I knocked on Reggie's door, and he led me to a classroom on the first floor. It was significantly smaller than the lecture hall in which our class had met. Instead of the long stationary tables, the room was filled with rows of individual desks, all empty save one.

"Ashley?"

She looked up from her test. Her hair looked cleaner, her

face less wan. She still wore sweats, but they seemed cleaner and the shirt matched both the pants and the scrunchy holding her ponytail in place.

She smiled. A thin smile, but a smile.

"I figured I ought to finish this stinkin' class and graduate before I have a kid to tote around," she said.

"Good girl."

Reggie directed me to a chair several rows away from Ashley and set my exam down on the desk.

"You have two hours," he said. "Do your own work. I'll check in on you occasionally."

I read through the test and answered the obvious questions, but I had a hard time concentrating. My mind had already jumped ahead to the logistics of the evening's event, and I found myself jotting down notes about how much Dublin Dr. Pepper I would need for the Pink Pepperberry milkshakes I was making for Crystal and Jason's wedding.

I forced myself to focus on the longer essay question, and was staring at the whiteboard at the front of the class trying to formulate my answer, when I noticed the faint writing there, the ghostly residue left from some class of yore. It looked like a language class of some sort, because the words weren't at all familiar.

Avec qui? Avec moi! Avec toi! Avec vous! Avec nous!

Avec qui?

I read the words over and over, something jarring loose in my poor, overstuffed brain.

Qui.

Of course! Q-U-I-T-A-M, the notation on Bryan's calendar. We'd all assumed it was "quit a.m." because those were words and phrases we recognized. English words and phrases.

But what if they weren't English words at all?

I looked at my test, then back at the board, then at my test.

The little voice in the back of my head that makes me drive the speed limit (almost always) and floss every day (religiously) was screaming bloody murder. I couldn't just walk out, without even trying to answer the test questions. That would be wildly irresponsible, even if I didn't have any real interest in the class in the first place.

I started writing, furiously, filling up several pages of a bluebook with an essay on themes of individual responsibility in Depression-era literature. I wasn't going to win any awards for my keen literary insight, but I did enough to quiet my conscience.

I closed the bluebook, tucked the exam inside, and dashed out into the hall.

Reggie was strolling back toward the classroom, his hands in his pockets.

"You done?"

"Yes," I said, handing him my exam. "But I have a question."

I grabbed him by the elbow and steered him to the doorway of the classroom. "That," I said pointing. "What does that say?"

He glanced down at me like I was a crazy person—which, in fairness, I surely seemed to be—but then squinted at the faint letters on the whiteboard.

"It's French," he said. "'With whom? With me! With you! With you! With us!' It's an exercise on pronouns."

"So what does q-u-i mean?"

"Who or whom."

"What about t-a-m?"

"My French isn't the best, but that's not a word I recognize."

"Huh. But qwee means who?"

He laughed. "Yes, but it's pronounced 'key'."

I felt like I'd been sucker punched.

That's what Emily had been saying the night she called. Not Tim's keys, but qui tam.

I still didn't know what it meant, but the answer was so close I could taste it.

Twenty-Seven

I briefly considered telling Finn what I'd learned, but I couldn't bring myself to raise his hopes again if this lead didn't pan out. It was still possible that Emily had been out of her mind, incoherent, that night on the phone. And I wasn't about to say anything to Cal until I had a suspect wrapped up in a nice pretty bow for him.

I had to put my bush league investigation on hold for the evening, while I got the fund-raiser taken care of.

The evening of the fund-raiser for the Bryan Campbell Scholarship, I about had a conniption. A Friday night in June, I had to leave the A-la-mode fully staffed, so I was on my own hauling ice cream cake to the Gish-Tunny Center. And, of course, the elevator was out, so I had to schlep the boxes of cake up two flights of stairs, taking them at a jog so the cake wouldn't melt before I got it into the freezer in the prep space behind the ballroom.

By the time the festivities got under way and I was able to turn over the task of plating the cake to Deena Silver's competent catering minions, I had worked up a bit of a sweat and had very little patience left.

Against my wishes, I was seated at the head table. I tried to finagle a seat next to Rosemary Gunderson, with the hope that we could pass the evening talking about our respective pets, but somehow I ended up between Cal and Jonas Landry. I had to restrain myself from physically recoiling from Jonas's presence.

Finn Harper, with his camera around his neck, lurked around the ballroom with a hangdog expression on his face. I got so tired of looking at his pitiful mug, that, between the salad and the main course, I pulled him behind a big potted ficus.

"What the heck is your problem tonight?" I hissed.

"I don't have a problem."

"BS. You look like someone just kicked your dog."

"I guess maybe I don't like seeing you all lovey-dovey with Cal McCormack."

I rolled my eyes. "First off, we're not lovey-dovey. I helped him plan this party, and now I'm sitting next to him. Big freakin' deal. Second off, I can get lovey-dovey with anyone I want, and I don't think you get to have a say. Heck, you're fixin' to leave Dalliance again, so what difference does it make to you what I do or who I see?"

"I haven't made a decision about staying in Dalliance yet. And I just don't want to see you make a mistake with your life," Finn said.

"Uh-huh. And dating a successful, law-abiding man would be a huge mistake."

"Cowboy Cal's got a poker so far up his ass he's gonna choke on it," Finn growled.

"You silver-tongued devil," I chided.

Finn colored, but he didn't back down.

"You know I'm right. You deserve better than that."

"That," I said with exaggerated emphasis, "is called being a grown-up. Something you could learn a little about, Finn Harper."

"Dammit, Tally, this isn't about being an adult. I take care of my own business, and you know it. But you need someone to balance you out, someone who'll take some risks and get you to move outside your comfort zone."

And there it was in a nutshell: Finn still saw me as a fixer-upper. With the right man in my life, I could be fun. But the woman I actually was, on my own two feet, played it too safe for Finn's tastes.

"Cal's not that man," Finn continued.

"And you are?"

He glanced away, just for a split second, but it was enough for me to see the indecision in his face.

Enough for me to know that Finn might have intentions, but he couldn't make promises.

"We were good together, Tally." He pulled me close to the lean length of him.

A tiny corner of my mind grumbled that it didn't feel quite right. This Finn had more muscle, more weight, more gravity than the Finn who held me all those years ago.

Maybe not quite right, but pretty darned wonderful. I had a second to get lost in the bracing clean of mint and evergreen and the delicious pressure of his hands on my back before he kissed me.

Twenty years fell away, and the teenage Tally wrapped her fingers around Finn's shoulders and held on for all she was worth. We were good together. So, so good.

Really. Good.

I couldn't form a coherent thought, but I didn't really need to. This, I knew. I felt. I did. I kissed him back with a passion I thought I'd lost.

I had my hands on the placket of Finn's shirt, pulling futilely at the fabric, when he came up for air. His face swam into focus, and what I saw there made my heart lurch.

Desire.

Very grown-up desire.

Somewhere nearby, someone dropped a dinner plate with an almighty clatter. I was suddenly painfully aware that I was tangled up with a man while over two hundred and fifty people tucked into chicken with apricot glaze and green beans amandine about ten feet away.

"Finn, not now," I said, pushing him away.

"If not now, then when?" he asked.

But he let me go.

The rest of the meal passed in a blur. I made small talk with Marla and Steve, both of whom thanked me for helping with the event. I felt guilty accepting their gratitude when I supported the woman they held accountable for their son's death. We all just wanted the truth, but I somehow felt like a double agent, a traitor to their cause.

And I did get a chance to chat with the Gundersons. George politely inquired after Alice, and looked disappointed that she'd had to work at the A-la-mode for the evening. The thought crossed my mind that the Gundersons taking a grandparently interest in Alice might be a good thing. They were cultured people, had connections outside of Dalliance, and, frankly, they had money. Knowing people like the Gundersons couldn't hurt.

The ice cream cake was a hit. I'd combined peanut butter, fudge, graham crackers, and marshmallow to pay homage to the peanut butter s'mores Bryan used to make when he went camping with his dad and Cal. It made Marla cry.

When the DJ announced Patty Loveless's "Blue Memories," couples swarmed onto the dance floor and slipped into the hold for the Texas two-step.

Cal pushed away from the table and offered me his hand. I took it, feeling my heart leap at the warmth of his skin. I caught the faint scent of leather and starch, homey, masculine scents that made me feel strangely safe.

We faced each other on the dance floor. He held on to my right hand, and placed his other hand on the curve of my waist. The two-step is not a close-up dance, yet that distance between us forced us to look in each other's eyes. The circle of our arms defined a private space, and his blue eyes held me there.

The tripping run of the guitar signaled the start of the dance, and the instant the lonesome cry of the fiddle filled the room, the gentle pressure of Cal's hand sent me stepping back, quick, quick, slow, slow, quick, quick, slow, slow.

I hadn't danced with many men in my life. Finn, of course. And a couple of awkward efforts with Wayne Jones. The occasional Dalliance civic leader at some function or another.

Dancing with Cal was different. He didn't have the innate grace Finn possessed, but he wasn't as stiff as Wayne. He led me around the floor without crowding or pushing. I retreated and he followed, relentless but patient.

"When I close my eyes," Patty sang, "I almost see the way you look when you were standing next to me." The words were filled with longing and regret, the music bittersweet. The song spoke to one man in my life, as another's heat enveloped me.

After a full turn around the dance floor, he spun me around beneath his arms so I ended up tucked against his side. As we promenaded, he leaned down to murmur in my ear.

"I didn't crawl out from under a rock, Tally. I know a little something about women. I understand why you might be attracted to Finn. He's fun, maybe a little dangerous, but he's not reliable." He spun me around into a classic hold and looked me square in the eye. "I am."

I nodded. I knew the truth of his words. Hadn't I relied on Cal in the past? Called him for help when my mama was too drunk to drive to the grocery store? Cried on his solid shoulder when Finn left town?

Quick, quick, slow, slow.

"I don't know what Finn can offer, but I'm offering you a life." He shifted us again, bringing me back to his side. "I'm offering you a steady, faithful man and maybe, God willing, a baby or two. Picket fence, PTA meetings, the works."

I stumbled, but his strong hands held me aloft, and we never missed a step.

"Are you proposing?" I gasped.

He pushed me away, then pulled me close, twisting us in a complicated and dizzying combination, before finally drawing me around to face him again.

Quick, quick, slow, slow.

"Is that so crazy?"

"Last year you were ready to arrest me for murder, and now you want to get married and have babies?"

He snorted, a sort of humorless laugh.

"Give me a little credit, Tally. There was a warrant, so I asked you to turn yourself in. I didn't want you to get hurt. But I didn't really think you killed anyone."

"Gee, thanks for the vote of confidence. But, Cal, where's this coming from? We've never even been on a date."

"Don't I know it! You always seemed way too young, and then before I made my move you started dating Finn. And when you broke up with Finn, I had already enlisted. By the time I got back, you were married." He spun me around once, disorienting me as I lost sight of him, but then he was there, filling my field of vision again. "The timing was never right, Tally, but I've been half in love with you my whole life."

"Half in love," I echoed. "But not all the way in love?"

The expression on his stern face never wavered, but his nostrils flared just a bit. I had come to recognize that tiny motion as a sign of annoyance. "Like you said, we've never even gone on a date. I'm not saying we should get married tomorrow or anything. I was just thinking we might go out. Court. Go steady." He laughed softly, as though surprised at his own whimsy. "We don't have to talk about anything legally binding until we've at least kissed a couple of times."

He started to spin me into another complicated turn, but I resisted, led us to the edge of the dance floor and to a halt. I pulled my hand away and cupped his hard jaw, his skin warm and slightly whiskery beneath my fingers. I melted a little when his eyelashes fluttered over his lightning blue eyes and he leaned into my caress.

Part of me thought, what the heck? It wouldn't hurt to go on a few dates with a handsome man, see where it led. But another part of me, the part that had been scorched by Finn Harper leaving me behind and burned by Wayne Jones's infidelity, that part of me sounded a warning bell. Cal made light of his mention of marriage, but did I really want to toy with a man so serious?

"Cal, what's going on here? What's brought this on?"

When he opened his eyes, I saw such pain and yearning there, I had to resist the urge to pull him into an embrace.

"I'm tired of waiting," he said simply.

"For what?"

"For the future. For the right time. For you. Bryan..." He trailed off and looked into the middle distance, composing himself. "This past month has made me realize how life can just"—his brow furrowed as he searched for the words—"just end."

He cleared his throat. "When I stood by his coffin, I thought about what he'd been doing the day he died, the humdrum little things he was doing that day, filling up what turned out to be the last minutes of his life, and it made me question how I spend my minutes. I don't want to waste any more minutes on waiting."

This time, I didn't even try to resist my impulse to pull him close. He folded around me like an old bed quilt, warm and heavy.

"Cal," I said softly, my voice muffled by the surprisingly soft skin beneath his jaw. "I'm so touched. But I've already had one ill-advised marriage. That's my quota. No more." He opened his mouth to protest, but I cut him off. "I think you need to get past your grief before you jump into anything, even just going steady."

I felt his whole body stiffen beneath my hand.

He pulled back. For a second, he wavered uncertainly, as though he might reach out and snatch me close again. But then he nodded his head once, turned on his heel, and stalked back to the table, drawing the anxious attention of everyone at the head table.

I let him go.

It was not a night for romance.

Twenty-Eight

I tipped my head back against the brick facade of the Gish-Tunny Center. The wall still held the heat of the afternoon sun, and the contrast between warm wall and cool air felt oddly comforting. I let my mind drift along the faint strains of music coming from inside, doing my best not to think about how my love life had gone from zero to sixty—and back to zero—in nothing flat that night.

"What are you doing out here?"

My eyes snapped open, and I found Bree and Alice standing before me, all clean and pressed and ready for a dance.

"Me? What about you?"

"Your friendly neighborhood Cinderellas have finished the housework and are ready to get their dance on," Bree replied.

I chuckled, but my heart wasn't in it.

"Can I borrow Alice for a minute or two?"

Bree gave me the stink-eye. "Are you going to get my child into more trouble?"

"I don't think so," I said hopefully.

"I'll be fine, Mama. I'll keep Aunt Tally safe."

"Okay. I'm going in to that dance to find some rich, handsome cowboy. But I've got my phone. Just buzz if you get in a pickle."

"Do me a favor," I said. "Tell Marla and Rosemary Gunderson that I'll be back in two shakes of a lamb's tail. I just needed to check something out across campus."

I took Alice by the hand and led her across the moonlit campus toward Sinclair Hall. "You still have Emily's keys, right?"

Alice nodded. "Are we breaking in?"

"No. Well, yes. But just to borrow her computer. We need to search the Internet for something."

We let ourselves into Emily's office, and Alice booted up the computer.

"What are we looking for?"

"Two words: q-u-i t-a-m."

She glanced up at me, her eyes wide with surprise, but then typed in the words.

"The very first result is for something called a qui tam action."

"Which is?"

"Um..." She clicked open a link and read to herself for a moment. "It looks like it's a type of lawsuit where an individual person sues on behalf of the government. So, like, if you found out that someone was cheating the government, by, like, charging the military too much for fighter jets, you could file a lawsuit representing the interest of the government."

She studied the screen some more, then uttered a short, mirthless laugh.

"Apparently the government wants to pay people to narc. So if you bring one of these lawsuits, you get a cut of whatever the government recovers. Like fifteen to twenty-five percent. And your attorney fees."

"Attorney fees?" I had a sudden thought. "Can you do a search for this type of lawsuit and 'attorneys' and 'Dalliance, Texas'?"

Her fingers flew over the keyboard.

"Huh," Alice said. "It looks like there's a directory of

lawyers in Texas who handle these types of cases. And there's only one listing in Dalliance: Jackson and Ver Steeg."

"Oh." I sagged against Emily's desk and closed my eyes. "Oh, my."

"What?" Alice asked.

Silence stretched between us, and I could almost hear the wheel click in her giant brain as she made the same realization I had.

"The difference between the two spreadsheets," she said. "It wasn't just a math error."

"No. Gunderson must have monkeyed with the spreadsheet template to calculate the facilities and administration charge using a slightly higher percentage. It padded all the grant requests by a bit, which he could then skim off the top. That's why Bryan told Ashley that fractions of percents mattered."

Alice whistled. "With Emily's grant, a fraction of a percent wouldn't amount to much, but for the hard sciences, those grants can be millions of dollars. Just half a percent of that is thousands of dollars."

"Bryan figured it out. And he decided to cash in, to file one of these qui tam actions. Probably because of the baby."

"But how would Gunderson have known?"

"Bryan's lawyer is Kristen Ver Steeg. Her partner is Madeline Jackson, who is Rosemary Gunderson's niece. I'm guessing Madeline Jackson said something to the Gundersons."

"She did."

Alice and I both yelped. We hadn't heard George Gunderson approach, and now he stood between us and the door. And he had a gun in his hand.

"She didn't mean to betray Bryan's confidentiality. She simply thanked us for referring Bryan to the firm and mentioned that he was considering a qui tam action, which could prove lucrative for the firm. It never occurred to her that I was involved in the fraud Bryan planned to expose."

George stepped further into Emily's office and shut the door behind him.

"It seems I misjudged you, Ms. Jones," he said. "I rather thought I might get caught, but not by you."

Was that a compliment? An insult? Did it really matter when I was clearly about to die?

"May I ask what gave me away?"

Fine. If the man wanted to play this game, I'd play, too. Anything to buy us a few more minutes, and maybe a chance of getting out of this pickle.

"Little things," I said. Beside me, I felt Alice shift in her seat, heard the faint click of her fingers on the computer keyboard. I kept talking to keep Gunderson's attention on me rather than her. "The pieces have been there all along—you had opportunity to kill Bryan, and you could easily hide the blood from your crime beneath your academic robes. Rosemary said you'd been working late, so you might well have run into Emily here the night she died. In fact, it was probably your tiramisu on the counter at her house. Between your wife and Ginger, you probably knew enough about insulin and diabetes to manipulate her sugar levels to incapacitate her until you could kill her. Then there were all the hints in what Bryan said and did before he died, comments about percentages and safe bets. You also seemed to have more money than other members of the faculty."

I shrugged. "I never would have put it all together, though, if I hadn't seen that French lesson on the whiteboard today. The night she died, Emily said something about a key, but it didn't make sense until I realized that she meant q-u-i, not k-e-y. And then, well, then it just fell into place," I concluded lamely.

George sighed. "Yes, Reggie mentioned you had been agitated about that French lesson. Still, you were perfectly pleasant at dinner. I thought perhaps you'd failed to connect the dots.   But then your cousin said you'd had a sudden inspiration and had hared off across campus.   It had to be something important to take you away from the party.   I knew then that you'd draw the inevitable conclusion." He shook his head sadly. "I didn't mean to do it, you know."

Was he serious? He stole tens of thousands of dollars over the course of years. Oops?

He squeezed his eyes closed and tilted his head, like he was trying to stretch out a stiff neck. Before I could take advantage of his distraction, his eyes popped open and he steadied the gun on me.

"I just, I need you to understand."

"I understand," I lied.

He laughed, a raw, desperate sound. "Anything to calm the crazy man? I'm afraid I'm not crazy, Ms. Jones. Just cornered. I'm not a bad man. I never wanted to hurt anyone."

Which would be cold comfort, indeed, to Bryan and Emily.

"Three years ago my Rosemary was diagnosed with breast cancer," he said. "You cannot imagine what it was like, holding her hand through the chemotherapy, holding her hair when she was sick and too weak to do it herself. My beautiful girl."

Despite the gravity of my situation, I felt a welling of emotion for this man, so obviously in love with his wife and so helpless in the face of her disease.

"God, the morning they wheeled her into the operating room for her surgery, she looked so small and frail in the bed. I wanted to go with her, to be with her, but she had to face it alone." He shrugged. "I was unmanned."

"She knew you loved her," I said.

"Yes, but love doesn't save your life. Medicine does." He shook his head tightly. "And then the bills started rolling in. I thought we had good insurance, but..." His voice trailed off.

"I couldn't let us lose everything, Ms. Jones. My Rosemary

had suffered enough. She'd supported me through graduate school, picked up and moved across the country when I got my first academic job, endured the loneliness of my pre-tenure years when I was consumed by work. When I traveled for my research, she stayed here, alone, in this backwater town and never once complained. The thought of her spending her golden years in poverty again, all because she'd married a man who loved ideas more than money...I couldn't let that happen."

"Of course not," I murmured soothingly.

"So I took some money. Just enough to cover the bills. I wasn't greedy. I just shuffled it from one bloated research account to another. Rosemary's happiness was worth more than a new computer that could solve a complex equation in thirty seconds instead of a minute."

I nodded again, but my attention had shifted to the door behind Gunderson. There was a tiny square window in that door, and I thought I saw a shadow move across it. If someone were out in the hallway, if I could just make a little noise, something to draw that unknown somebody's attention without startling George.

"I took the money, and then I had to find a way to give it back. Eventually, those accounts would be audited. The researchers would wonder where their money went. That's when I got the idea to pad the budgets up front. I only planned to fiddle with the percentages until I'd paid back the money I borrowed. But once I started, it was just so easy to keep doing it. And it meant I could take better care of Rosemary. We could afford help around the house, and I could take her on trips."

And to eat regularly at the Hickory Tavern. I kept my lips shut. My mama didn't raise any fools, and I wasn't going to poke back at the man with the gun.

"I know it was wrong, Ms. Jones. If it were only my life on the line, I would have turned myself in when Bryan Campbell discovered what I'd been doing. I never would have paid him any blackmail money, and I certainly wouldn't have killed him when he threatened to expose me anyway."

Out of the corner of my eye, I caught a flash of movement. The door?

"But it isn't just my life," George continued. "It's Rosemary's. She's strong, stronger than I, and she could withstand the scandal. But I would have to pay back the money. They would take everything to get their pound of flesh: our house, Rosemary's jewelry, our savings, everything. She'd be left with nothing. What if the cancer came back? How would she fight it, alone, without any money?"

I heard a faint scraping sound. Someone had definitely slipped into the room. I didn't dare look to see who it was, though.

Another sound, a squeak of rubber on linoleum, faint but clear. George twitched, and started to turn, as though he, too, had heard the noise.

Quickly, I tried to distract him.

"I see how it happened, Professor Gunderson. One small lapse in judgment, and then years covering it up." In my peripheral vision, I saw the door behind Gunderson inch open. "The problem growing bigger and bigger," I rushed on. "You didn't mean to, but once you started, there was no stopping it."

Something flared in his eyes—joy, relief, excitement? "Exactly," he exclaimed. "One small lapse in judgment..." He laughed softly. "The poet was correct. 'Oh, what a tangled web we weave when first we practice to deceive!'" His gaze sharpened on me. "Do you know who said that?"

Really? This hardly seemed the time for a quiz. I went with the old standby. "Shakespeare?"

"Sir Walter Scott."

Gunderson and I both jumped nearly out of our skins and

spun around to find Bree standing at the back of the room. She stood perfectly still, her hands open and spread away from her body to show that she wasn't armed.

Her eyes met mine briefly, and she must have seen the shock in my face. She arched a brow and drawled, "What? I can read, you know?"

I don't know whether it was Bree's sudden appearance or her startling command of British literature that knocked George off guard, but I took full advantage of his momentary confusion. I grabbed the first thing I encountered—Emily Clowper's flea market Styrofoam rooster—and threw it at Gunderson with all my might.

The rooster bounced off him, doing no real damage, but he threw up his arms in a defensive reflex.

Bree, too, snatched the nearest object, a much more weapon-worthy book from on top of Emily's filing cabinet. She threw it overhand, and it struck Gunderson squarely in the forehead.

He stumbled and the gun went flying.

Alice scrambled over the desk, lunging for the gun, while Bree and I both tackled Gunderson.

We had him pinned to the ground, groaning, and Alice was standing on top of Emily's desk with the gun trained on Gunderson's head, when Cal and Finn came rushing into the office.

Cal, his weapon drawn and a look of panic on his face, surveyed the scene.

"Lord-a-mighty, I've had nightmares like this."

Beside him, Finn laughed. "Me too. But in mine, a couple people were naked and the rooster was very much alive."

Twenty-Nine

I didn't see Cal or Finn during the week between Gunderson's arrest and Crystal and Jason's wedding. Finn's articles about ivory tower corruption—Jonas Landry's fabricated interviews and George Gunderson's massive embezzlement—made national news, and Cal fielded media requests from across the state. I just wanted to lay low and wait for the dust to settle.

But in a town the size of Dalliance, you can't avoid anyone for very long, and we were all at the wedding at the Silver Jack.

A whip-thin young man in a tux, a black cowboy hat, and silver-chased boots ushered Deena down the flower-lined aisle. She had the poor boy's arm in a death grip, and he had to pry her fingers from his sleeve to hand her off to Tom Silver. A gentle murmur of laughter rippled through the guests, and then they grew silent when Crystal Tompkins stepped through the French doors and onto the patio.

She stood in the midst of her pink-ribboned bridesmaids, swathed from head to toe in silk chiffon, a circlet of palest pink tea roses anchoring a gossamer veil to her sleek cinnamon bob. One by one, her friends paired off with dapper cowboys to mosey down the aisle, until Crystal stood alone, her chin high, her bouquet of lilies and roses clutched to her breast.

As she crossed the lawn and swayed down the aisle, the honeyed light of late afternoon caught the flecks of gold in her amber eyes. She looked like a voluptuous fairy engulfed in a cloud of dandelion floss. She took my breath away.

I tore my eyes away to watch her groom's face. He had the dazed look of a man crawling out of a lifeboat onto dry land. At one point, he rocked forward on his toes and I thought he might bolt down the aisle to greet her. But he held his ground until she stood at his side, gazing up at him with the sure knowledge of her power over him.

Beside me, I heard Bree snuffle. She always cried at weddings. Especially her own.

Beyond her, I heard a muffled groan from Alice, who had her mother's tender heart but lacked her sentimentality.

Mother and daughter had been clingy for a few days after our tussle with George Gunderson. Alice's quick thinking, using her e-mail account to send her mother a text message for help, and Bree's Amazonian book-throwing skills had created a sense of mutual admiration. But, of course, that had melted away after a week, and we'd returned to a familiar state of mother-daughter detente.

I turned my attention back to the bride and groom. They were pledging their undying love to one another, in sickness and in health, for richer or for poorer.

I couldn't help but think of George and Rosemary Gunderson. He'd stood by her in sickness, and now she was standing by him in poverty, their assets frozen as authorities sought to determine the extent of his theft.

So much pain, all in the name of love.

It was almost enough to make me swear off romance forever.

Almost.

After the service, the bridal party disappeared for a round of photographs, while the rest of the guests convened in the barnyard for cocktails and the signature Pink Pepperberry "groom's shakes" we were serving.

I drifted through the sea of guests, passing out champagne flutes filled with luscious deep pink milkshakes. Finn, documenting the day on film, nearly backed over me twice. Both times, he offered me overly polite apologies. The second time, I felt tears well in my eyes.

I finished my circuit, handing my next to last flute to one of Crystal's sorority friends, and then wandered over to greet Cal McCormack. He stood off to the side of the yard, at the fringes of the party, and he nodded in greeting as I approached.

"Truce?"

Cal squinted hard and studied me from tip to tail before dusting his hand on his pants and holding it out for me to shake. "Truce."

I let his big fingers close around my smaller ones, felt the sinew and strength of his grip. He made me feel fragile and girly. Not a bad feeling, mind you, but one I had no business feeling at that precise moment. I forced my lips to turn up in a teasing smile. "Aren't we supposed to spit on our palms or something?"

He leaned in close, bringing the scent of leather and line-dried laundry with him. "Nah. I can think of better ways to swap spit if that's what you've got in mind."

My breath caught and a furious burn licked up my cheeks. "Cal McCormack!"

He chuckled, a low and liquid sound like water at the bottom of a well. "Settle down, Tally. I'm just teasing." He winked. "Probably."

I handed him the last flute of milkshake, and he accepted it with a gentlemanly nod of the head. He took a tentative sip.

"Delicious," he said, a bemused smile on his face. "What's in it?"

I smiled back. "Raspberries, for one. And a secret ingredient known only to the bride and groom."

No one other than me, Jason, and Crystal knew that the

milkshakes contained a Dr. Pepper reduction, which added a rich complexity to the bright note of the berries. I'd even managed to keep Bree in the dark. Not only was I worried about how Dr. Pepper-flavored ice cream would be received, but I figured Jason and Crystal would enjoy sharing a secret on their wedding day.

"I can taste the berries, but there's something else there. Familiar, but I can't place it." He shrugged. "Whatever it is, it's tasty. Reminds me of you. Sweet, but not simple."

I felt my face heating up at his compliment, and guessed I was probably every bit as pink as the milkshakes.

I suddenly realized we were still holding hands right in the middle of the Silver Jack barnyard. I began to pull away, but just then the band inside the barn struck up "When the Saints Go Marching In," and folks started pairing up for the Grand March.

Cal tugged me around so I stood at his side and dragged me to a spot in line right behind the groom's parents. I craned my neck looking for Bree, hoping I could get her to take my place, but I watched in dismay as she shoved Alice and Kyle together and then pulled Finn into the line right behind us.

Ahead of me, the line started moving, everyone stomping their feet and shaking their hips in time to the music. When Cal started forward, I followed dutifully, but I felt the force of Finn's gaze on the back of my neck.

We shuffled through the barn doors and into the reception site. Fairy lights and flowered garlands hung from the rafters and the oak plank floor glowed a mellow gold in the gentle light. Long trestle tables topped with crisp white linens, colorful mismatched china, and dozens of ivory pillar candles lined either side of the big open space. A dozen or so of the older folks were already perched on the benches, nodding their heads and tapping their toes to the beat. The flower girl, one of Jason's nieces, snuggled on the lap of one plump matron, her white patent leather Mary Janes peeping from the frothy pink spill of her skirts. The woman clasped the child's hands in her own and clapped them gently together.

Two by two, the bridal party and guests danced down the length of the barn. At the front of the room, the couples peeled off, alternately moving to the right or the left, forming two lines that boogied around the perimeter of the room and back to the door. There, the two lines merged again as each couple met another and formed a group of four.

Cal didn't have the best sense of rhythm, but he bopped along good naturedly, swinging our joined hands back and forth between us.

Ahead of me, I watched as Tom and Deena Silver met the Arbaughs, coming from the other side, in front of the barn door. Deena took Mr. Arbaugh's hand in her own, and the foursome began the trek down the dance floor again.

Cal and I rounded the corner and came face to face with Bree and Finn. Cal stiffened just slightly, and I hesitated a beat before taking the last few steps and reaching out for Finn's hand. To their credit, neither man came to a full stop. Casual observers might not have even noticed the tension between them.

But I noticed, and I was caught squarely in the middle.

Finn, the passion of my past. Cal, with his promise of respectability and stability. Just exactly what I'd always wanted.

If I'd figured out anything over the last year it was this: you have to live in the now.

As I stood between those two men, one like fire, the other like rock, I realized I needed to focus on who they were at that exact moment. Who I was at that exact moment. How they made me feel.

And I knew which man held my heart at that very point in time.

My heart pounding in my chest, I squeezed his hand.

WENDY LYN WATSON

Despite some serious temptation, the only thing Wendy Lyn Watson has killed so far is a pint of ice cream. Well, pints. Plural. A lot of them.

When she isn't tasting her way from chai ginger chip to balsamic strawberry to Mexican vanilla, Wendy teaches American government and constitutional law to college students. She lives in a completely neglected historic home in North Texas with the most patient man in the world and the Tabby Congress (Tiberius, Blaze, and Squeak-a-Doodle). Between teaching, writing, volunteering with the Modified Dolls, and more, life is busy but the cherry on every single sundae.

**The Mystery A-la-mode Series
by Wendy Lyn Watson**

Henery Press Mystery Books

And finally, before you go...
Here are a few other mysteries
you might enjoy:

THE AMBITIOUS CARD

John Gaspard

An Eli Marks Mystery (#1)

The life of a magician isn't all kiddie shows and card tricks. Sometimes it's murder. When magician Eli Marks very publicly debunks a famed psychic, said psychic ends up dead. The evidence, including a bloody King of Diamonds playing card (one from Eli's own Ambitious Card routine), directs the police right to Eli.

As more psychics are slain, and more King cards rise to the top, Eli can't escape suspicion. Things get really complicated when romance blooms with a beautiful psychic, and Eli discovers she's the next target for murder, and he's scheduled to die with her. Now Eli must use every trick he knows to keep them both alive and reveal the true killer.

Available at booksellers nationwide and online

Visit www.henerypress.com for details

PUMPKINS IN PARADISE

Kathi Daley

A Tj Jensen Mystery (#1)

Between volunteering for the annual pumpkin festival and coaching her girls to the state soccer finals, high school teacher Tj Jensen finds her good friend Zachary Collins dead in his favorite chair.

When the handsome new deputy closes the case without so much as a "why" or "how," Tj turns her attention from chili cook-offs and pumpkin carving to complex puzzles, prophetic riddles, and a decades-old secret she seems destined to unravel.

Available at booksellers nationwide and online

Visit www.henerypress.com for details

A MUDDIED MURDER

Wendy Tyson

A Greenhouse Mystery (#1)

When Megan Sawyer gives up her big-city law career to care for her grandmother and run the family's organic farm and café, she expects to find peace and tranquility in her scenic hometown of Winsome, Pennsylvania. Instead, her goat goes missing, rain muddies her fields, the town denies her business permits, and her family's Colonial-era farm sucks up the remains of her savings.

Just when she thinks she's reached the bottom of the rain barrel, Megan and the town's hunky veterinarian discover the local zoning commissioner's battered body in her barn. Now Megan's thrust into the middle of a murder investigation—and she's the chief suspect. Can Megan dig through small-town secrets, local politics, and old grievances in time to find a killer before that killer strikes again?

Available at booksellers nationwide and online

Visit www.henerypress.com for details

BONES TO PICK

Linda Lovely

A Brie Hooker Mystery (#1)

Living on a farm with four hundred goats and a cantankerous carnivore isn't among vegan chef Brie Hooker's list of lifetime ambitions. But she can't walk away from her Aunt Eva, who needs help operating her dairy.

Once she calls her aunt's goat farm home, grisly discoveries offer ample inducements for Brie to employ her entire vocabulary of cheese-and-meat curses. The troubles begin when the farm's pot-bellied pig unearths the skull of Eva's missing husband. The sheriff, kin to the deceased, sets out to pin the murder on Eva. He doesn't reckon on Brie's resolve to prove her aunt's innocence. Death threats, ruinous pedicures, psychic shenanigans, and biker bar fisticuffs won't stop Brie from unmasking the killer, even when romantic befuddlement throws her a curve.

Available at booksellers nationwide and online

Visit www.henerypress.com for details

70588619R00136

Made in the USA
Middletown, DE
27 September 2019